2

Th
lat
pe

•
•

McGRAW RETURNS

Twenty years in prison tamed Jack McGraw, or so he thought. He returns to Crockett, Texas, where he meets his daughter, Rebecca, for the first time, and discovers that he must save her and their farm from Ben Page. Unknown to Rebecca, Page has found crude oil on an unused part of the farm. A sample sent to Pittsburg confirmed its value, and Page alone knows it's worth millions. He sends his henchmen to kidnap Rebecca, and soon McGraw finds himself on a three-state rescue mission . . .

Books by J. W. Throgmorton
in the Linford Western Library:

TOOTS McGEE

J. W. THROGMORTON

◆

MCGRAW RETURNS

Complete and Unabridged

LINFORD
Leicester

First published in Great Britain in 2015 by
Robert Hale Limited
London

First Linford Edition
published 2018
by arrangement with
Robert Hale
an imprint of
The Crowood Press
Wiltshire

A catalogue record for this book is available
from the British Library.

ISBN 978–1–4448–3597–7

Published by
F. A. Thorpe (Publishing)
Anstey, Leicestershire

Set by Words & Graphics Ltd.
Anstey, Leicestershire
Printed and bound in Great Britain by
T. J. International Ltd., Padstow, Cornwall

This book is printed on acid-free paper

Prologue

The lanky young man watched close as the cards slid from the faro box.

'I don't like the way them cards are comin' out of the shoe,' said Jack McGraw. 'Too many pairs turned.'

The din at the faro table dropped to a hushed silence, and everyone stared at the dealer, a slight-built man in a white linen suit. His dark eyes glared hard at the young man as he stroked his moustache with a crooked finger. His hands were soft and delicate — almost feminine. Finally, he sneered, 'That's big talk, sonny, for someone not heeled.' His smile turned icy, and his dark eyes even colder.

Jack's steel-blue eyes flashed with anger. 'You sayin' them cards ain't stacked?' He leaned forward with his hands pressed on the table's green baize as he posed to rise.

1

Red Thomas dealt faro at the White Elephant Saloon for the better part of two weeks. He'd pegged the local gamblers as yokels not smart enough to catch on to his brand of cheating. This young fella, however, appeared to have seen the elephant before and wasn't to be shown again.

Red had to back him down, or else he'd get run out of town, or maybe worse. It was Red's habit to take careful notice of any man who sat at his table. So he knew the young man was unarmed. His intent was to send him packin' with his tail tucked between his legs. Red reached across his chest to pull his hideout gun, a .41 Remington Derringer. Its accuracy was questionable beyond fifteen feet, but from across a faro table it was deadly.

No one was more surprised than Red; before the Derringer cleared Red's coat, as if by magic, the young man had filled his left hand with a .45 Navy Colt. Red saw three flashes erupt from the pistol's octagon barrel a split second after he felt the jabs to his chest. His arms went limp and dropped to his sides. When he tried to stand, he hadn't the coordination or strength to make it happen, his legs kicked out away from his chair. His expression was of everlasting surprise; things had gone horribly wrong. He slumped forward on the table, dead.

The other five players at the table, two ranch hands and three local businessmen, scrambled out of the way when the fracas began. After the shooting stopped and the smoke cleared, one of the cowboys yelled, 'Damn, he's done kilt Fingers.'

It didn't register with Jack at first who the cowboy meant, then Jack looked past the gambler and saw Fingers, the piano player, on the floor. Two red splotches grew on the front of his white ruffled shirt. Two of the three rounds had passed plumb through Red Thomas and killed Fingers.

The townsfolk liked Fingers, and most people enjoyed listening to him play the piano, but that was the extent of his talents and the only thing he knew how to do. He was known to stand in the rain and wonder why he was wet. When the argument started, he selected the unoccupied location behind Red for a better view of what was about to transpire. He didn't seem the least bit curious as to why he stood alone.

Jack didn't run; he sat quietly and waited for the sheriff. Red had gone for his gun first, while Jack was unarmed. If the man next to him hadn't already loosened the holster's keeper loop on his hog-leg Colt, it'd be Jack lyin' on the table.

Fingers's death was an accident, pure and simple. Jack figured he'd have to spend the night in jail. Just until the sheriff got things sorted out, but he didn't expect anything more; certainly not what happened next.

Dallas, Texas, was a Confederate town during the War, but the Yankee Carpetbaggers ran things now; they weren't about to let a Johnny Reb get away with killin' two men over a card game. So they bound Jack over for trial.

Even the carpetbaggers had to admit that killing Red Thomas was self-defence, but Fingers was another matter. Fingers was well-liked, and many would miss his piano playing at the White Elephant. The jury settled on aggravated manslaughter, and the judge sentenced him to twenty years at Huntsville Prison.

1

Jack McGraw stuffed the last of his meagre belongings into an old black satchel. Its condition spoke to years of unmaintained storage. The bag, once supple and shone a burnished lustre that gleamed in the light, was now a brittle shell of dried-out and cracked leather. In a way, he felt it served as a metaphor for his life. He gazed solemnly at the bag he'd carried to Dallas so long ago; if he could change history, he would've stayed home with his wife and unborn daughter in Crockett, Texas.

A crooked grin spread across Jack McGraw's face as he looked at Kurt Jager, his cellmate, friend, and mentor; he gestured to the bag. 'It's not much to show for the last eighteen years of my life, is it?'

Kurt, who wanted to lighten the

sombre mood, placed a hand on Jack's shoulder. 'The clothes they gave you fit a bit tight. I'd say all these years here, doing farm labour, have made you bigger, certainly harder.'

The prison issued Jack two pairs of socks to wear with his hardly used black laced boots, a brand new pair of denim trousers, a cotton shirt, and a jacket made from indigo-coloured wool. Six foot two and broad-shouldered, Jack puffed up and crossed his arms to stretch the clothing across his back; the seams held.

'They aren't as good as the ones I wore when I arrived, but they'll do 'til I can afford to buy better.'

Kurt reached into his pocket and retrieved an object. He held it up. It was the king's paladin; the knight. 'I want you to have this as a reminder that you've always got more than one option. I chose the white; they make the first move. After you leave this place, you'll have a lot of moves to make. I hope you choose correctly, and that I never see you again.'

Jack studied the object in his friend's hand; he knew Kurt carved it from a piece of maple secreted from the wood shop. He formed its shape with a broken piece of glass and bleached it white using lye soap from the prison laundry. Its subsequent satin-smooth honey colour came from years of handling.

He and Kurt spent innumerable hours playing chess. It took Jack more than a year to achieve his first stalemate and nearly two for a checkmate against his friend. Jack's brow and eyes drooped as he forced a smile for his friend.

'Kurt, I can't accept that, you spent years carving those pieces.'

Kurt chuckled. 'I've got plenty of time to carve another.' He reached out and took Jack's hand and pressed the piece into his palm. 'It's also something to remember me by — '

'I don't see how I'd ever forget you. We've spent every day together for the last eighteen years.' Jack let out a half laugh. 'Hell, that's a longer run than most marriages.'

'I don't think many couples would survive day in and day out in these close quarters. One's sure to kill the other,' said Kurt, and they both laughed. For a moment, Kurt seemed to forget why he was serving a life sentence in Huntsville Prison.

Kurt's crime of passion happened the year they opened Huntsville for business. He and his new bride, Emma, emigrated to east Texas from Germany two years earlier. Kurt, who was older, spent his time, and a large portion of his energy at working their farm. Though he wasn't demonstrative, he nonetheless cherished her and naïvely believed she did him.

Emma, who was forced into the marriage by her father, resented being made to leave her friends and family. There were other German emigrants in the area, but none nearby. The farms were larger in north-east Texas than back in Germany, so socializing was difficult. Their closest neighbour was the Eichel family, whom Emma visited often while Kurt worked the fields.

The Eichels' oldest son, Dolf, who was two years younger than Emma, was smitten by her beauty. It started harmlessly enough, but before long their flirtations became a heated romance.

Oblivious to what was happening, Kurt came home from a buying trip earlier than expected and caught them in the throes of making passionate love. He flew into a jealous rage and threw himself on to Dolf. Not a large man, but nevertheless a strong one, he beat young Dolf to death with his bare hands.

Emma, whose naked body glistened with the sweat of their lovemaking, and wet ringlets of hair clung to the nape of her neck, stood in the corner of their bedroom, clutching a sheet to cover her exposed womanhood. Kurt often wondered, had she not provoked him with her words, if he would he have still killed her, too. He liked to think not.

Each word she spewed enlivened Kurt's rage as he approached her. Hunched forward, stalking like a crazed bear, his hooded eyes stared at her with the vilest of hatred.

'You've killed him! They'll hang you for murder, and I'll finally be rid of you and this godforsaken farm.' He continued forward. 'Do you hear me?'

He tore away her sheet, but she refused to cower. With her hands on her hips, she glared at him defiantly. Only in his nightmares did he remember the details of killing her. When his senses returned, he placed their battered bodies on the bed, covered them, and turned himself in to the sheriff.

Dolf's father was a very powerful man in the community. So instead of manslaughter, they convicted Kurt of first-degree murder and gave him a life sentence.

Jack looked on as he saw Kurt's eyes cloud with the memory of Emma. 'Sorry, Kurt, I didn't mean to bring up — '

'Weren't your fault, Jack, besides, I'm not the only one to lose his wife.' He paused and studied Jack for several seconds. 'You still plannin' to see your daughter?'

'Yup, I do,' said Jack, and a huge smile spread across his face and forced his cheeks up to crescent his eyes. It always pleased him when they talked about his daughter. Though he was yet to meet her, Rebecca, whom her grandparents named after her mother, had become the centre of his world.

'What're you goin' to do about your wife's parents?'

Jack's smile vanished. He looked down at the packet of yellowed letters from his wife and the one on top from her father, Herman Gottlieb. He'd received the news of Rebecca's pregnancy with mixed emotions. Thrilled that she was pregnant, but depressed that he couldn't be with her. His only solace was that she still had her parents to take care of her.

Later, it came as a terrible blow when

he read that Rebecca died giving birth to their child. In the same letter, Herman and Dora also explained that they intended to raise his daughter as their own, and he wasn't ever to darken their door. Jack fell into a dark depression, and for a while, he became a dangerous prisoner. Not caring if he lived or died, he confronted the most lethal inmates in Huntsville. It was then that he met Kurt, who saved his life and showed him a better, quieter way to live.

'I've not figured that out as yet. I reckon I'll just play it by ear and see how things go when I get there.'

Kurt put a hand on Jack's shoulder. 'You're not the same man who entered here eighteen years ago. Maybe they'll see the change and welcome your return home.'

Jack smiled, but it held no humour. 'We'll see — '

The stout, ham-handed prison guard named Murphy tapped his billystick on the bars. 'It's time, McGraw. The warden's waitin' — you've got to see him before you're released.'

Jack extended his hand to Kurt. When he glanced down and saw the contrast in their clothing, he hesitated. The difference was unsettling; Kurt's black and white stripe versus his indigo sleeve, it seemed strange for his clothes to be so dissimilar.

'Goodbye, Jack. Please write when you get a chance.'

Jack nodded and turned to leave; he paused and said over his shoulder, 'Would you believe it; some part of me is goin' to miss the security of this place.'

'You're not the first,' said the guard. 'Maybe that's why so many of you come back — it's home.'

'Not me, Murphy — I've got a home, and that's where I'm goin'. I've got a lot of lost time to make up to my daughter.'

'I've heard that before, too,' said the guard, smacking his palm with the black billy to emphasize his statement.

Jack didn't reply. It seemed pointless.

He glanced back one last time at his cell mate and friend, who gave him a smile and a wave. 'So long, Jack, don't forget to write.'

In front of Superintendent Goree's desk, though it'd been twenty years since he'd been in the military, McGraw stood at something akin to a parade rest. He wanted to show his respect to the once confederate officer.

Assigned as General James Longstreet's aide during the Civil War, Thomas Goree, by all accounts, acquitted himself bravely during battle. Since he assumed authority for Huntsville Prison, he'd instituted numerous programmes to improve conditions. Many of his reforms were designed to rehabilitate instead of punishing the inmates; some actually learned a trade.

A stern-looking, clean-shaven man with reported strong Christian values, Goree busied himself with the papers on his desk. He didn't immediately respond to McGraw's presence. At length, he glanced at McGraw.

'According to these documents, you're being released today.'

'Yes, sir,' said McGraw as he snapped to attention.

Goree recognized the response. 'You served in the War?'

Small curves appeared at the corners of McGraw's mouth. 'Yes, sir, Second Cavalry, Company E.'

Goree glanced at McGraw's file. 'You were one of the young ones — '

'Yes, sir, Captain.' McGraw grinned.

'It says here you were convicted of manslaughter.'

'Yes, sir. I was at the wrong place at the wrong time.'

Goree studied McGraw for several seconds. Finally, he said, 'Stand easy, McGraw. By all accounts, your record here has been exceptional. I'm curious — tell me about the 'wrong place'.'

McGraw stood at ease; his eyes lost their focus as he remembered the fight. 'I was in Dallas on business. Things had gone well, so I decided to celebrate a little and went to the White Elephant

17

Saloon for a drink.' He paused to look at Goree, who nodded for him to continue. 'Well, sir, one drink led to too many and a faro game. The dealer was a cheat and I called him out.' He stared off into the past. 'He pulled a hideout gun and I shot him three times in the chest.'

'Was three times necessary?' asked Goree.

'Well, sir, during the War more'n one soldier was killed by a Yankee thought dead — I learned to make sure.'

'In retrospect, maybe you should have left your gun elsewhere while you celebrated.' Goree added an under-standing smile.

'I wasn't heeled, sir.' Goree raised his brow. 'The fella on my left was, so I yanked his pistol — '

'It says here,' Goree pointed to his file, 'that you're right-handed. I'd say that's pretty good shootin'.'

'My mother pushed me to favour the right, but I can use either one just as good.'

Goree nodded. 'It sounds more like self-defence to me, why'd they convict you on manslaughter?'

McGraw's face fell. 'The piano player standin' behind the faro dealer — two of the three slugs passed through, and killed him.' He shrugged. 'Everyone in town liked him, so I got twenty years.'

Despite the circumstances, Goree saw humour in the situation and smiled. 'It was hard luck all around, son. What are your plans when you leave here?'

The grin returned to McGraw's face. 'I have a daughter, she lives in Crockett and I aim to see her, sir.'

Goree scowled. 'I meant how do you plan on makin' a livin'?'

'Oh,' said McGraw. 'I guess I'll go back to farmin' — that's all I really know how to do.'

The superintendent's expression hardened. 'I'd say you learned some skills in the army. See to it that you don't go to usin' them again. I'd hate to see you back here scheduled for a hangin'. You get my meanin', McGraw?'

McGraw snapped to attention. 'Yes, sir, I do — you won't.'

'Avery,' called Goree to the guard. 'We're done. Process Mr McGraw and see he makes it to the train depot.'

Avery cast a quick glance at McGraw. 'Yes, sir, Captain.' He took McGraw's arm and led him out of Goree's office. Outside, he said, 'You must be special. The Captain's never instructed me to make sure anyone got to the train depot before.'

2

'Crockett, Crockett, Texas. Next stop is Crockett, Texas,' called the conductor.

McGraw, who'd been dozing, opened his eyes and looked out of the window. He expected changes, but he didn't recognize anything he saw through the rail car's window. He caught the conductor's sleeve.

'You sure this is Crockett?'

The conductor jerked his arm free and glowered at McGraw. 'I've been stoppin' here three times a week for the last three years. Nothin's changed — it's Crockett. You gettin' off?'

McGraw nodded, stood, stretched the kinks from his back, grabbed his cracked leather case, and made his way to the passenger car's exit. Clouds of steam swirled as the train's brakes released and pulled away. He stood on the platform and watched. He felt deserted; the train was his only lifeline to the here and now — and carried a reality he could identify.

Minutes passed. Soon, he was the only person left on the platform. The station attendant, a jovial acting man, came out of the depot and asked, 'Can I help you, sir?'

McGraw's first impulse was to look about to see who the attendant was addressing. He checked his action, and instead asked, 'I need a horse, where's the livery stable?'

The attendant pointed. 'East end of town past the new courthouse; just stay on Goliad — you can't miss it. Matthews's — it's on the right.' He smiled. 'Tell John that I sent you, he'll reduce the rental price.'

McGraw nodded, tucked his travel-worn satchel under his arm and started walking towards the town. The court-house's clock tower became his reference point. It amazed him at how the town changed. Last time he'd been to Crock-ett, the courthouse was built out of logs;

timber being so readily available. It doubled as a fort when the Indians raided. This new courthouse built of blue limestone looked pretty damn impressive in comparison. On passing the courthouse, he saw the Pickwick Hotel.

McGraw smiled at the signs painted on the three-storey building. Wm. Berry, Owner, was nearly as large as the hotel's name.

The station attendant was right; Matthews's wasn't hard to find. There was an unwashed, sorry-looking, old fat man standing outside the livery. McGraw asked, 'Is Matthews around?'

The short round gent pulled a blue hanky from his Levis, pulled off his filthy sweat-stained hat, and wiped his partially bald head and neck. 'I'm Matthews.' He squinted against the sun's glare. 'What do you want, young fella?'

Jack smiled at the idea of him being addressed as a youth. 'I need a horse and tack.' He glanced at the corral to his left. 'The man at the depot said to tell you he sent me.'

Matthews hooked his thumbs behind the leather suspenders and exposed bright red stripes on his otherwise sun-faded long-johns. He stepped closer and stared at McGraw squinty-eyed; he smelled of horses and manure.

'That'd be Ben, my sister's oldest boy. I 'spect he told ya I'd give ya a good price.' McGraw nodded, and the old gent chuckled. 'Well, I'm the only stable in town.' Matthews paused to push the frayed ends of his sleeves up. 'So, any price I quote is a good'un.'

McGraw kept his expression pleasant. There was nothing to be gained by having words with Matthews. 'Which are for sale?'

The old man gestured at the corral, walked towards the gate. 'All three of 'em mares is fer sale — take your pick.'

The horses shied away when McGraw opened the gate and entered the corral. He stood still and waited. A sorrel, more curious than the other two, walked over to investigate the man who stood in the

centre of the corral. The dun with intel-
ligent eyes was the one he was interested
in. A lot changed since he'd gone to
prison, but horse flesh remained the
same.

'There ya are — ' said Matthews, his
smile revealing lost teeth. 'She likes ya
— it's important to have your horse like
ya.'

'How much?' asked McGraw as he
stroked the sorrel's neck.

The old horse trader's smile increased
to a grin, he knew the animal wasn't
worth more than thirty dollars.

'Fifty dollars — '

McGraw remained pleasant. 'It's
been a while since I bought a horse, but
still, that price seems high.'

'Well, son, I tell ya, that horse surely
has taken a likin' to ya, and since you
seem like a nice fella, I'll take five
dollars off the price.'

Still stoking the sorrel's neck and
ignoring the other animals, McGraw asked,
'How much are the other two?'

Matthews's squinty-eyed stare returned

as he studied McGraw, trying to divine his intentions. Finally, he said, 'Them horses is all priced the same — fifty dollars. You can take your pick.'

'Does that include the tack?' asked McGraw.

'I reckon it does. There're two old saddles in the barn, you can have whichever one ya want.'

McGraw grinned, walked over and offered his hand through the fence. When Matthews accepted, McGraw said, 'I'll take the dun.'

'But that ain't the one we been talkin' about.'

Still smiling, McGraw said, 'You said they were all priced the same and I should take my pick.'

'But that dun's the best of the three, she's worth fifty or more.'

'Yes, sir, Mr Matthews, I agree. I'll need a bill of sale for forty-five and note the rigs included.'

Matthews gave McGraw his squinty-eyed stare for several seconds. He considered backing out of the deal, but in the end decided to honour his word.

The old gent chuckled, 'I guess it don't hurt for folks to know that I was out-traded by a farmhand.'

McGraw ferruled his brow. 'What makes you say farmhand?'

'Why, it's plain to tell from your red neck. Wearin' a hat don't do ya much good when you're bent over all day. Look at the way you stand — tall and straight. If you worked from a horse, you'd be bow-legged.' Matthews nodded. It was easy to see that he was pleased with his estimation of Jack McGraw. 'Yes, siree, you're used to the hard life of farm work. If you're lookin' for work around here you'll likely find it.'

While Matthews went to write up the bill of sale, McGraw saddled the dun. When he finished, he walked into the office.

'What can you tell me about the Gottlieb family?'

Matthews stiffened. 'What's your business with them folks?'

The sudden hostility in Matthews's

tone made McGraw suspicious. So he pretended not to notice, and said, 'Friends of the family suggested I looked them up while I'm here.'

'Well, sonny, you're too late. Dora Gottlieb died two years ago, and Herman cashed in about six months back.'

McGraw choked back the urge to question the old man about Rebecca and turned away so as not to let Matthews see the concern in his eyes. 'Is that bill of sale ready?'

'Huh — ' Matthews stared at McGraw and finally understanding shone in his eyes, and he looked down at the paper in his hand. 'It's right here — where's my fifty dollars?'

'Here're two twenty dollar gold pieces and five greenbacks. The bill of sale had better state paid in full.'

The old skinflint chuckled. 'You can't blame a body for trying to earn a fair dollar.'

With his horse and tack secured, McGraw's next order of business meant a stop for supplies. He glanced up at the sign: *Simpson & Son Dry Goods & Hardware.* The last time he entered the store, it was just Simpson's Dry Goods, and the building constructed of timbers. Now the building was built of stone with a tin roof and twice the size.

McGraw recalled Simpson was about his age and wondered if the storekeeper would remember him from years ago. Inside the store, McGraw saw goods and doodads, which he thought of as more at home in Saint Louie. The storekeeper nodded to acknowledge McGraw's presence. Simpson remained lean; his already prominent nose seemed longer than McGraw remembered, but his close-set beady eyes were the same. He still had the off-putting habit of twitching his nose like a rat between his sentences. Aside from that, he remained a friendly enough cuss, who kept an eye on the townsfolk and liked to gossip.

The store was empty save McGraw. As he approached, a warm smile spread across the storekeeper's face.

'Howdy, stranger, how can I help you?' If Simpson recognized him, he didn't show it.

McGraw returned the smile. 'I need to pick up a few things.'

As Jack wandered through the store and selected items for purchase, they fell into a friendly conversation. With McGraw's display of interest in what Simpson had to say, it didn't take many questions to find out what happened to the Gottliebs.

'Dora Gottlieb contracted a cancer. It affected her female parts.' Simpson paused to shake his head and sadness clouded his eyes. 'She took a long time dying, and it were painful, too. It durned near drove Herman mad havin' to watch her die like that. It's no wonder he took to drinkin'. It took him a while, but he finally joined her six months back.'

Finally, McGraw asked Simpson the question that most concerned him. 'What about their daughter?' He held his breath as he waited for Simpson to give his answer.

'Why, the poor thing — she's still out there on the farm trying to manage the best she can.' His nose twitched. 'Ben Page, he's a saloon owner, offered to buy the place from her, but she's been stubborn about acceptin'.' Simpson leant in, smiled, and lowered his voice. 'I think Ben's sweet on 'er.'

McGraw released his breath; he felt weak with relief and placed his hand on the counter. Despite the difficulty, he forced himself to remain composed, and said, 'You don't say — '

'Yes, siree, Bob — why, every time Miss Rebecca comes to town, Ben's in here moonin' around her like a puppy. She don't pay him no mind, though, but it ain't stopped 'im from tryin'.'

'You say this Page owns a saloon?' asked McGraw.

'Yup, the Timber Saloon — it ain't as nice as the Pickwick, but it'll do for a drink and faro if you're of a mind.'

'Timber, I've heard a lot of names for saloons, but — '

Simpson chuckled. 'I know what you

mean. His grand-daddy, Ben Vaughn, had a daughter who married a fella from Pennsylvania, I think it was. They named their boy after old Ben, so a few years back, when Vaughn died, he left young Ben a huge stand of tall pines; which he sold and made hisself rich. When he bought the Broken Spoke, he changed the name.'

'I don't gamble, but I could use a beer — which way?'

'It's a block over.' He gestured south with his thumb.

'Thanks.' McGraw paid for and gathered up his purchases. 'I'll be seein' ya,' he said over his shoulder as he left.

3

Like most of the newer buildings in Crockett, the Timber Saloon was constructed of stone and sported a shiny tin roof. McGraw peered over the batwing doors. The smell of stale beer and tobacco assaulted his sense of smell. It'd been a long time since he'd stepped into a saloon; it took a few seconds to adjust. He pushed through the doors and walked to the far end of the bar. In the shadows, he'd go unnoticed and could watch the men in the room as they mingled or drank.

A deep building, the saloon's bar ran the length of the room with a row of tables across from it. There were two doors in the back, one led to a storage room, and the other an office. If there was a back door, he guessed it'd be through the storeroom. Oil lamps along the wall hung over the tables and reflected in the mirrors behind the bar; it was dark and gloomy, the kind of place a man came to, to be alone and drink in peace.

McGraw scanned the faces of the men in the room.

'What'll you have?' asked the bartender. Jack turned to see who spoke. The man whose pock-scarred and unshaven face made him appear markedly unfriendly asked, 'Well — beer or whiskey?'

'Beer,' said McGraw quietly. He didn't make eye contact. It was something he learned in prison from Kurt — 'Don't be confrontational, and you won't be remembered.'

It was early afternoon; with few patrons, the bar was quiet. The faro table had two players plus the dealer; two other men sat at a table near the doors, and four leaned on the bar. McGraw sipped his beer and waited. His patience paid off; thirty minutes later, a blond-headed dandy pushed through the doors, paraded the length of the room, nodded to the lanky bartender, and entered the office.

Page, he thought, *not much to look at. He seems like a dude, if ever I saw one.* Then, he recalled the mistake Matthews made with his appearance. He clinched his jaw. *I'll not make that mistake.* He ordered a second beer and prepared to watch and listen; he wanted to learn more about Mr Page.

On his third beer, he began to feel its effects. He'd not had alcohol for eighteen years; plus he'd not eaten since his arrival. When the bartender neared his end of the bar, he asked, 'Can a fella get something to eat here?'

The bartender paused as if considering. Finally, he sat a plate with a block of cheddar cheese covered with a towel and a tin of soda crackers in front of McGraw. 'Help yourself.'

The cheese was hard; he wasn't sure that it was still good, but the salted soda crackers were heartily welcomed by his stomach. He must've eaten twenty by the time the bartender returned.

'Another beer?' he asked.

McGraw glanced at his glass, it was half full. 'No, thanks,' he said and smiled at the bartender. 'The crackers were good.'

The bartender covered the cheese block and closed the cracker tin, and returned both back under the bar.

He'd just about given up on the idea of waiting, when Page came out of his office and stepped to the bar.

'Whiskey, Sam,' he said to the bartender.

Sam reached under the bar, where the crackers were stored, and retrieved a bottle of Canadian-bonded whiskey.

'Here ya go, boss,' said Sam as he poured a glass and sat the bottle down.

Page turned, facing the room and rested his elbows on the bar's edge. 'Business is slow today, Sam.' Sam didn't respond, it was something Page said every day when he came out of his office. Looking around the room, Page laid eyes on McGraw. He said, 'You're new in town — stayin' long?'

McGraw allowed a brief smile and

replied, 'Hadn't made up my mind yet. I'll be needin' to find work if I stay.'

'Well, if you know anything about timber, the loggers are always lookin' for men — tough work, though.' Page studied McGraw for several seconds. 'You the fella that bested Matthews in the horse trade?' he asked. His curiosity seemed real.

'I paid a fair price for my horse — wouldn't say I bested him.'

Page laughed; he appeared genuinely entertained. 'If you got a fair deal from Matthews, you bested him all right. Let me buy you a whiskey.' He lifted the bottle and nodded to Sam, who fetched another glass from the shelves behind the bar.

McGraw held up his hand. 'Thank you, but I ain't got much tolerance. If I drank some of your whiskey I'd fall off my horse.'

Page nodded, his smile said he wasn't offended. 'Maybe next time.' He saluted McGraw with his glass and finished his drink.

Coming out of the saloon, McGraw brushed shoulders with a man entering.

'Watch it, if you know what's good for you,' said the man as he turned to confront McGraw. Recognition flashed in his eyes, and the man said, 'That you, Jack? I'll be damned — it is you. When did you get out?'

It was Billy McCarthy, a young ne'er-do-well, and who served ten years at Huntsville for armed robbery. Billy didn't have enough gumption to be on his own. McGraw glanced outside to see who he was with. Billy was alone. In a quiet voice, McGraw said, 'I'd just as soon you didn't advertise my bein' in Huntsville.'

Billy looked around to see who'd heard, only Page paid any attention. Billy said, 'Sure thing, Jack. Let me buy you a drink for old time's sake — no hard feelings.'

'Maybe later, Billy. I got some business to attend to.'

'Sure thing, Jack,' said Billy, and he turned to enter the saloon. McGraw watched as he went to the bar and stood next to Page. Their conversation seemed immediate and hushed. It was none of McGraw's business, so he headed for his horse.

4

Jack sat atop his dun and surveyed the farm. It looked much the same as when he'd last been here, except now it appeared tired. He saw signs of neglectfulness. The barn's once bright red was now a dirty rust colour like that of dried blood. The corral needed repairs, and the gouged out arch in the dirt told him that its gate dragged the ground.

'Please state your business.' The young woman's question broke his concentration. When he turned to the sound of her voice, his face sagged and his mouth fell open. For an instant, no more than a split second, he saw his Rebecca. In his mind, she looked exactly like her mother. The same creamy complexion, dark hair, and expressive brown eyes; cow's eyes he used to tell his wife.

He suppressed the impulse to leap from his horse and rush to scoop the tiny young woman up into his arms.

'Well,' said the young woman, 'what's your business here?' She emphasized her statement with the barrel of the shotgun tucked under her arm.

McGraw removed his hat and smiled. 'Lookin' for work, ma'am — the name's Jack McGraw.' He watched her face closely with the hope of seeing a sign of recognition at hearing his name. Her expression never changed. He continued, 'Man down to the store said you might be hirin'.'

He lied about Simpson. Nonetheless, it was true; Rebecca needed help desperately. He held his breath and waited as she considered the situation.

Rebecca studied the man's face. There was something familiar about him, but she couldn't quite put her finger on what it was. She decided to trust her instincts. Though she hadn't actually pointed it at the stranger, she lowered her shotgun.

'I can't pay much, but I'm a good cook, so you won't go hungry. There's a lot of work. Things have gone to seed since my pa died.'

Her last words caused a sharp pang of sadness, but he inhaled deeply to cover the hurt.

'Beggars can't be choosy,' he said, still smiling. 'Just show me where to hang my hat, ma'am.'

'Please don't call me ma'am. My name is Rebecca Gottlieb — you may call me Miss, um, Rebecca will be fine.'

'Thank you, Rebecca. Where do I sleep?'

She pointed. 'There's a room in the barn. It has a wood stove and a bed — when you come to the house for supper, I'll have your bed linen ready.' She turned to go back to the house, but stopped and looked back. 'You've not asked about your wages?'

Jack, who'd dismounted and was walking away towards the barn, halted, looked over his shoulder and said, 'I figure you'll be fair and pay what you can.'

She stared after him until he entered

the barn; she shrugged and continued on into the house. *It'll be nice to have someone around here to help out . . . and talk to*, she thought. Again, she was struck by the odd feeling that she could trust Mr McGraw.

Inside the barn, Jack saw just how neglected the chores were. His first job would be to muck the stalls and see to the mules. Without healthy animals there'd be no farming. He put his belongings into the bunk room, unsaddled the dun, and released her into the corral.

The details of the farm slowly returned. In the lean-to shed at the back of the barn, he found the wheelbarrow and tools needed to clean the stalls. When Rebecca called him for supper, he'd only completed one stall.

'I'll be there in a minute. Let me wash up a bit first.'

She waved, and he grabbed a bucket, filled it, and went around to the side of the barn where a wash-up station waited. The mirror, now twenty years older, was cracked and some of the silver flaked off its back, but he could still see his reflection; he was smiling. Then it occurred to him; he was happy. It was the first real joy and contentment he'd felt in eighteen years.

The aroma of home-cooked food reached him halfway to the house. Rebecca met him at the door and showed him where to sit. Inside, he saw what looked like a feast to him: ham, peas, greens, fried potatoes, and fresh-baked bread. Rebecca had been busy, too. He stood by his chair until she was seated. He poured a glass of tea, and forked a slice of ham and raked off some potatoes.

'Ahem.' He looked up and Rebecca stared at him. She said, 'It's my habit to say Grace before a meal.'

Sheepishly, Jack lowered the platter. 'Too long on the trail — a man develops bad habits. It won't happen again, Rebecca.'

She smiled and bowed her head; Jack did the same. When she finished, he returned to loading his plate, but reminded himself he wasn't in prison where eating a meal was a competition.

Rebecca watched Jack as he ate in silence, his eyes focused on his plate. She decided that if they were to have a conversation, she'd have to be the one to start.

'What brings you to this part of Texas, Mr McGraw?'

Jack's arm froze mid-bite. He hadn't expected her to ask him questions. Finally, he looked up and said, 'I've lived in Texas, one part or another, most of my life. East Texas is greener than the rest — good for growin' things; suits me better.'

She smiled, hoping to encourage more information, but that was all he would say.

'So, you've farmed a lot?' she asked.

He nodded as he chewed his bite, and then washed it down with a swallow of tea. 'I was raised on one — don't know that I know how to do anything else.'

'Well, this place needs work. I thought — '

He cut her off. 'I've started with the stalls, next I'll see to the mules, and then repairs and painting. When spring comes, we'll be ready for plantin'. There's tobacco seed in the barn, they're a good cash crop.'

She stared at him. 'You seem to have everything planned. Do I have a say about anything?' Her tone was ripe with sarcasm.

He realized his mistake. 'Sorry, Rebecca, I didn't mean to take over like that — it's just that the things need doin' are sort of plain to see, and I — '

Her smile returned. 'You're right, Mr McGraw. You tend to the chores as you see fit. We'll discuss the crops later — we've time.' She glanced at his plate, he'd cleaned it. 'I've dessert — peach cobbler, if you're interested.'

After dinner, he took a second helping of the cobbler and coffee to the bunk room. There were two sets of bunk beds and a single bunk by the door where he sat at a makeshift desk. *This must be for the foreman, if they ever had one*, he thought. He chuckled to himself as he said aloud, 'Well, I'm in charge of the farm's labour force, so I guess it must be for me.'

Jack scraped the plate but there was some cobbler still on it. He foolishly looked about, and just like a little boy, he licked it clean. She was right about being a good cook.

Satisfied and feeling happier than he could remember, Jack pulled off his boots and lay back on the bunk. He drifted off to sleep without making the bed.

5

Daybreak and the rooster's crowing came much too soon. After stretching to discover which of his tired muscles hurt the most, he rolled off the bed. The bedding still piled where he left it.

'I suppose I should make the bed before I start the day, or it might not ever get done,' he said aloud.

He milked the cow and took the bucket to the house. Rebecca was up and cooking breakfast. She glanced at the bucket when he entered.

'That's my chore. I do that and feed the chickens after breakfast.' She again looked at the milk tin and saw the amount. 'Sally's generally not so generous, you must have the touch — she's picky about who milks her, too.'

'I've always gotten along with children and animals,' said Jack. 'It's the adults that give me trouble.'

Rebecca smiled at the comment, but saw that he was looking elsewhere and there was no humour in his eyes. She started to ask him what he meant, but thought better of it, and she turned back to the stove to see to the biscuits.

She served him a hearty breakfast. As he finished his coffee, she said, 'You're a pleasure to cook for. I've never seen anyone clean a plate the way you do.'

Jack gave her a genuine smile. 'I've learned to appreciate good cookin' and eat all I can get when I can get it.' He stood to leave. 'Those chores won't do themselves — '

She called, 'Come to the house mid-morning, and you can have the last of the cobbler.'

He waved; she saw his ears rise and knew that he grinned.

Rebecca and Jack quickly fell into a routine. McGraw continued to be elusive about his more recent past, though he did tell her stories of his youth that made her laugh. For her part, she spoke freely about herself and her life on the farm.

' — it was bad after Ma died; Pa took it hard and started drinking. He wasn't mean or anything, just sad. Soon the farm began to show his neglect.' She paused to wipe the tears that began to spill down her cheeks. 'And then Pa died.'

Jack still felt a pang when she called Herman Pa, but he didn't let it show. He sat silently and waited for Rebecca's moment of grief to pass. Finally, she took a deep breath.

'Sorry, it's just that I miss them so much.'

'I understand,' said Jack, nearly giving in to the impulse to comfort his daughter. Instead, he stood to leave the kitchen. 'I've just about got the barn's roof mended. I'd like to finish, before it gets dark.'

She smiled and nodded. As he left, he heard her blow her nose and then dishes clink; she'd recovered.

The roof repairs were on the back side of the barn, so he couldn't see the house, but he heard horses trotting into the yard. He climbed to the barn's ridge and looked down. It was Billy McCarthy and an older man, near Jack's age.

Rebecca stepped through the screen door out on to the porch. Jack could see that from her posture and tilt of her head that she wasn't pleased to see them.

'Billy, you tell Page that my answer remains the same. My farm is not for sale — that's my final word. Now get off my property.'

'That's not very friendly,' said the older man as he dismounted. He passed his reins to Billy and stepped to the edge of the porch. 'Maybe someone should teach you some manners.'

'Take it easy, Frank. You heard Page, no rough stuff.'

Frank sneered over his shoulder at Billy. 'I see why he's sweet on her. She's a good-lookin' little filly — though a bit uppity.' He reached out and snatched her off the porch and before she could resist, he kissed her on the mouth.

McGraw had climbed down from the roof and stood in the shadows of the barn. When he saw the older man grab Rebecca, he bolted out from the barn with an axe handle in his hand. Several things happened all at once. Frank returned Rebecca to the porch; Jack's sudden approach spooked the horses; Billy's bucked him off; and Jack swung the axe with all his strength at Frank's knee. The breaking bone was audible, followed by Frank's scream.

Billy scrambled to his feet and went for his Colt, but he was too late. Jack was on him with the axe handle. As Billy pulled the revolver, Jack struck his wrist, shattering the bones. Both men lay on the ground moaning. With Billy's Colt in his hand, Jack knelt beside the one called Frank and cocked the hammer.

Adrenaline pumped fiercely through Frank's veins and blocked the pain of his broken leg.

'Don't shoot, mister. I didn't hurt

her. It was just a kiss — I was funnin', that's all.'

'Jack, please don't hurt him further,' pleaded Rebecca.

Billy was now on his knees, cradling his right arm. He hadn't seen who attacked them, but now that he did, he was amazed.

'McGraw, I thought we were friends, why'd you go and do this?' He gestured with his right elbow which caused him to wince. 'I think my wrist is broke.'

Jack exhaled deeply, releasing the rage he'd felt. 'You shouldn't have gone for your Colt,' he said. He placed the end of the axe handle on Frank's chest and pinned him to the ground. 'This *hombre* is the one that needs to learn some manners.' Jack reached down and took Frank's pistol.

Their horses had settled and stood nearby. Jack brought the animals near and helped each man to mount. Frank glared at Jack, and asked, 'What about our guns?'

'I'll leave them with the sheriff on my

next visit to town.'

Assured that Jack wasn't going to kill him, his bravado had returned. 'You'd better come heeled — '

Jack held up the axe handle. 'I don't think I'll need anything more'n this to deal with the likes of you — now git.'

As he spoke, he moved towards them, and when he held up the handle, their horses shied away and bolted into a gallop. He watched them until they were out of sight, before he turned back to Rebecca.

'Are you all right?' he asked.

She was pale and hugged herself as if she were cold. 'Yes, I think so.' Her voice trembled with fear. She'd never seen such violence, certainly not on her front porch. 'Would you have killed those men, Mr McGraw?'

He stared at her for several seconds. He could see that she was frightened of him; something he deeply regretted.

'Only if they'd forced me to,' he said. 'Something I learned in the War, if you make a half-hearted attack you'll likely lose. If I'd given them boys a chance, they'd have killed me and claimed self-defence. Now they know I mean business. I doubt they'll return.'

Rebecca watched Jack as he spoke. His blue-grey eyes were calm. At his temples, she noticed for the first time, streaks of white, as he finger-combed his hair back before putting on his hat. His voice held no rancor; it was as if he were explaining something about the farm. Slowly, her concerns abated.

'At least those two won't come back,' she said.

McGraw asked, 'Those two?' His stare was a question.

Rebecca sighed and sat on the porch steps. Jack joined her and waited. Finally, she began to speak. 'It's Ben Page — he wants me to marry him so he can take over my land. He's chased off my workers and every so often sends men out here to try to frighten me. I guess he thinks if I've no other choices, I'll give in and marry him, but he's wrong.'

'What's he after? It's a farm much like the others nearby.'

Rebecca shrugged. 'I really have no idea. All the fertile land is being farmed. The only other property is the outcropping on the east side of the farm. Snakes and critters is all it's good for. The marriage proposals started after I refused to sell.' She gave an impish grin. 'I tried flirtation to find out, but he wouldn't tell me why he wants the place.'

'Have you talked to the sheriff?'

'Yes, but I've no real proof, so it's his word against mine. Page is an influential man around Crockett, so — '

'I can testify about what happened.'

Her eyes remained sad, but she forced a smile when she turned to face him. 'Is the roof done?' she asked.

He smiled. 'Maybe an hour's work to finish.'

'I'll have supper ready by the time you've completed.' She turned quickly, lifted her skirt to see the porch steps and bounded across the porch into the house.

6

A week and a half passed after Billy McCarthy and Frank came to the farm. It was Saturday, and Rebecca wanted to go to town to restock the kitchen and do some shopping.

McGraw hitched two of the mules to the farm's buckboard, and they headed for Crockett right after breakfast. It was the first day free of chores for McGraw in nearly a month.

Outside of Simpson's store, McGraw hopped down from the wagon, toting a flour sack containing Billy and Frank's weapons.

'I'll take these to the sheriff's office and tell him what happened.'

Rebecca nodded absently as she looked down the street. 'I'll leave the supplies list with Mr Simpson. If you need me I'll be at Millie's dress shop.'

She climbed down from the wagon

before Jack could walk around to help her. He smiled at her excitement as she marched into the dry goods store.

Sheriff John Clark, a clean-shaven rawboned man of forty, sat at his desk filling out paper work. He glanced at McGraw and then down at the flour sack that landed on the corner of his desk with a clunk.

'What can I do for you?' asked the sheriff.

'You can return these to Billy McCarthy and his pal, Frank.'

A glint of mirth shone in Clark's eyes. 'So you're McGraw? Billy says you attacked them with an axe handle without call.'

McGraw sized up the sheriff as a fair-minded man, and asked, 'What does Frank say happened?'

Clark grinned. 'That's the funny part. Frank says he was never there and that his horse threw him and broke his leg.'

'Where do we go from here, Sheriff?'

Clark reached across his desk and

dragged the sack back to his lap. 'Well, I tell ya. Frank fell off his horse, and Billy ain't filed a complaint, so I guess it ends there.' He opened the sack and placed the revolvers on his desk. 'I'll return these — Billy won't have any use for his for quite a spell, but Frank will want his for sure. You — um, I mean his horse, ruined his knee. He'll drag that leg permanently. Frank's the type to carry a grudge, and I've pegged him for a back shooter. I'd arm myself were I you.' The springs creaked as Clark rocked back in his chair 'What'd they do anyway?'

'Miss Gottlieb has made complaints.' Clark nodded. 'The older one, Billy called Frank, physically accosted Rebecca. I stepped in with an axe handle. Billy pulled on me — I was quicker.'

Clark exhaled slowly and shook his head. 'I suspected it was somethin' like that, which is why Frank wants to let it drop.'

McGraw's stare hardened. 'I'm a witness to what happened, what are you going to do about Page?'

The sheriff threw his hands outwards, palms up. 'There's not much I can do. Page asked Miss Gottlieb to marry him, and she said no. Other than an occasional tipped hat and 'Good morning', that's all he's done. I can't prove otherwise.'

'I saw Page and McCarthy together at the saloon a few days before he showed up at the farm,' said McGraw.

'Unless you can prove they were plannin' somethin' illegal . . . '

McGraw's furrows deepened on his brow. 'Maybe I'll have a talk with Page and explain it ain't right to rough up women.'

'I can't tell you not to talk to him,' said Clark, 'but if you hit him that's assault and I'll have to arrest you.'

'What if it's self-defence?'

'In this town, McGraw, it would still be assault.'

McGraw leaned on Clark's desktop. 'So, you're owned by Page?'

Clark jumped up from his chair, his

face an angry red, and his eyes glared. 'McGraw, there ain't no one holding nothin' over my head exceptin' the laws for the State of Texas.' He exhaled forcefully as if trying to blow away his anger. 'What I meant was, regardless of who swings first everyone in this town, except me, will swear you assaulted Page. It's that simple.'

'Well then, Sheriff, you can go with me.'

'If I did and you lost your head, I'd have to arrest you.'

The grim slit of McGraw's mouth softened to a sarcastic smile. 'I've had lots of practice at controlling my temper.'

Clark pulled his watch from his pocket and released the catch. The cover flipped up; McGraw studied Clark as he paused to stare at the picture before checking the time. 'It's past noon and a beer would make this a better day.'

'I noticed the picture — family?' asked McGraw.

'Yeah.' Clark's expression saddened. 'Wife and daughter, I lost 'em two years back to the fever.'

'Sorry, I understand your loss.'

Clark glanced at McGraw. 'You had a family?'

McGraw's jaw clinched. 'I lost my wife eighteen years ago givin' birth to our baby girl and my daughter a few days later.'

Clark didn't respond with words, but the solemn look in his eyes expressed everything necessary. 'Come on, I reckon Page'll be at the Timber.' The sheriff headed for the door.

With McGraw following, he and Clark entered the Timber Saloon. Frank, his leg splinted and propped in a chair, and Billy, his arm in a sling, sat at a table next to Page's office door. They exchanged glances when they saw McGraw with Clark.

At the bar, Clark said, 'I'll have a beer, Sam.' After the bartender sat his drink on the bar, he added, 'Where's Page?'

The bartender nodded towards the office door. McGraw, who stood beside Clark, said, 'Tell 'im there's someone here who wants to have a word with 'im.'

The bartender looked at Clark.

'Better do what he says,' said Clark. He threw a glance at Billy and Frank. 'They're proof you don't want to aggravate the man.'

Sam got a glimpse at Billy and Frank, and the bartender's eyes grew large. He looked back at McGraw. 'Yes, sir,' he said, and hurried away to tell Page that McGraw was waiting.

Ben Page glanced at Sam when he entered his office.

'I'm busy, Sam, what is it?' Sam didn't answer right away, which was unusual. Page put down his pen and looked up to consider his bartender and saw Sam's uneasiness. 'What's wrong, Sam?'

'McGraw, the man that busted up Billy and Frank, is outside with Sheriff Clark, and he wants to talk to you.'

A sudden grin sprang to Page's face. 'If Clark's with him there won't be any trouble. Tell them I'll be out shortly.'

'But, Ben.' Sam was reluctant to face McGraw again. Page might not be in danger, but Sam wasn't so sure.

Page's expression hardened. 'Go on and do as I say, Sam.'

Feeling trapped, he nervously twisted the bar towel between his hands. The only dampness it held was the sweat from his palms.

'Yes, sir,' he said and inched out of the door.

Sam returned with Page's message.

Clark ordered another beer. He wasn't sure if it was the alcohol on an empty stomach, or that he was tired of Page running things in his town, but he began to feel happy. If Page braced McGraw and there was a fight, he wasn't all that sure he'd arrest him; besides, he was startin' to like the big galoot. He finished his second beer just as Page came out; he tapped the glass for another.

'Mr McGraw, to what do I owe the honour of your visit?' Page offered his hand as he approached.

McGraw studied him closer this time. The man was soft; it was obvious that he had others do his work. His pale blue eyes showed no character. Jack noticed the tip of his left earlobe was gone. It was a clean cut; could it have been from a knife fight? McGraw didn't take his hand. Page looked down at it awkwardly, and then clasped it together with his left.

'I'm sure your men told you what happened at the Gottlieb place.'

Page glanced over his shoulder at Billy and Frank. 'They are patrons of this establishment, nothing more. I am aware, however, that you assaulted them with an axe handle.'

McGraw's expression was deadpan. 'Did Frank there tell you he was manhandling Miss Gottlieb and that's why I stepped in?'

Page's blank expression wavered. It was a few blinks of his eyes and his jaw slightly clinched, but McGraw saw it. Billy and Frank hadn't told Page all the facts; they'd have things to explain later. Of that, Jack was sure.

'Why, no, he didn't. That sort of behaviour is deplorable, but why should I care? Was Miss Gottlieb harmed in any way?'

'A little bruised. It's her pride and sense of security that's hurt most; that's where I come in.' He leaned in close. 'Any more men show up at the farm, or if you cause Miss Gottlieb any further trouble, I'll take it up with you personally.'

Page stepped back and smoothed his clothes. 'I'm not sure I understand what you mean, are you threatening me?'

'Not at all, Page; I'm makin' you a solemn promise.'

Page's face blanched. 'Sheriff, are you going to just stand there and let this ex-convict threaten me?'

Page's comment caught Clark, who'd enjoyed the spectacle thus far, off-guard. He asked, 'That right, McGraw

— you an ex-con?'

McGraw never took his eyes off Page. He stared hard at him so Page would know the words were directed at him, and he said, 'That's right, Sheriff; I killed a man for lookin' at me wrong.'

The beer had gone to Clark's head; he saw the situation as funny and laughed. 'You're pullin' my leg. They would've hung you for that in Texas — what'd you really do?'

Despite McGraw's feeling towards Page, Clark's incredulous manner made him smile. 'I accidently killed a piano player while I was killin' a cardsharp that was cheatin' me.'

Clark, who forgot why McGraw originally came into the Timber Saloon asked, 'So you killed a man who cheated you? If the piano player was an accident, why'd you go to prison?'

'Carpetbaggers liked the way he played,' answered McGraw.

'Hell, he must've been some piano player,' said Clark.

McGraw began to wonder how the

conversation drifted away from why he came in here in the first place. 'Look, Sheriff, the piano player was well-liked, but it had more to do with my serving in the Confederate Army than the piano player.'

'You've served your time,' said Clark. 'As long as you don't cause trouble in Crockett, you won't have a problem with me.'

McGraw's smile vanished as he again focused on Page. 'I guess it's up to Page if I become a problem. If he stays away from Rebecca Gottlieb and her farm, I'll be a model citizen.'

'Sheriff,' bellowed Page, 'I demand you arrest this man for making threats of violence.'

'Threats ain't against the law, Page. Now if he assaults or kills you, you can rest assured the law will take action.'

McGraw found himself grinning. 'I've had my say, Sheriff. Thanks for watchin' my back.' He turned away from Page and walked out of the Timber. As he pushed through the batwing doors, he heard Page sputtering threats at the sheriff.

McGraw paused on the boardwalk to survey the street. Across the street, he saw Robert Simpson had finished loading the wagon. The storekeeper raised his hand to shade his eyes. He stared at Jack for several long seconds, and then turned his attention down the street. Jack followed Simpson's gaze, and he saw Rebecca outside the dress shop. He glanced back to Simpson and saw the storekeeper again stare at him; it was more than a casual glance.

Rebecca talked with a young man not much older than she. He was tall and fencepost thin; McGraw noticed the revolver that hung low from his hip, and that it was tied to his leg. As they talked, the young man worried the brim of his hat with fingers like an old woman with her Rosary. McGraw smiled at their behaviour. Rebecca stared at the young man as if he were candy. Neither of them heard his approach.

'Ahem,' said McGraw.

Startled, they both jumped. Rebecca put a hand to her throat as she gasped. The young man's hand dropped to his gun. McGraw grinned.

'Sorry, Rebecca, I didn't mean to spook you.'

Rebecca offered a smile, and said, 'We should've paid more attention.' She glanced from the young man at Jack, who watched the young man. 'Mr McGraw, this is John Simpson.'

'You related to the storeowner?' asked Jack.

'Yeah, he's my pa.' John's tone had an edge to it, and he stood more erect as if challenged.

'Your pa seems like a good man, John,' said Jack as he offered his hand. 'You know, my name's John, too, but everyone took to callin' me Jack on account of my pa's name being John, too.'

John didn't take the offered hand. 'My pa's given name is Robert — he don't like it none when folks call him Bob.'

'Folks can get mighty peculiar about their names.' Jack looked at Rebecca who watched John. 'I don't mean to crowd you two, but there's chores waitin'. I'll be at the wagon.'

Rebecca said, 'I suppose you're right — I'll be along.'

As Jack walked away, he heard John say, 'If he works for you, then he can't tell you what to do, Rebecca. Stay in town for a while. I'll buy you dinner and take you home later.'

Jack slowed his pace to listen. 'John, I own a farm, and it doesn't work itself. Besides, Jack's been a Godsend, and if he hadn't been there when Page's men showed up — '

'What're you talkin' about?' John's voice sounded concerned.

'Billy McCarthy and an older man came by the farm a while back.' She saw John's jaw tighten and paused.

'Go on, tell me what happened.'

'It's been handled, John, I don't — '

'Rebecca, please tell me what happened.'

'Well, in the past they've just harassed me and ran off my workers, but this time the older man, Billy called him Frank, held my arms down and kissed me. Before he could do more, Mr McGraw stepped in and — ' She shrugged.

John's glance shot to the Timber Saloon. 'So that's why. They told it like your man attacked them for no reason.' His hand dropped to his gun butt. 'If they wasn't already busted up — '

Rebecca grabbed John's gun arm and tugged to pull his hand away from the Colt. 'John, please don't do anything rash. It was only a kiss. Mr McGraw more than punished them enough.'

He let go of the Colt and watched McGraw as he walked towards the wagon. In a lowered voice, John said, 'You know he's an ex-con?'

Rebecca stiffened and stepped back, and then she looked after McGraw. 'I don't believe it — there must be a mistake.'

'Well, it's true. Billy spent time with

him at Huntsville.'

'I'm sure there were extenuating circumstances,' she said.

John patted his Colt's handle and gave her a cocky grin. 'You want me to come out to your place and send him packin'?'

Rebecca's eyes flashed. 'No, it's none of your affair.' She hiked up the front of her skirt and marched after McGraw.

She passed Jack and climbed onto the wagon before he reached her to offer a hand. Jack heaved himself onto his portion of the seat and slapped the reins to get the mules headed for home.

For a long while, Jack and Rebecca rode in silence. Finally, she said, 'John said you spent time in Huntsville prison.' She hesitated then continued, 'Was it for something very bad?'

He let out a sigh. 'I guess it was just a matter of time. I wanted to tell you about it myself, but the right occasion — '

'You can tell me now. I think I have a right to know.'

McGraw told her about the shooting, and about the carpetbaggers railroading him into prison. As for Rebecca's mother and her, he only said prison cost him a family.

'I've changed since that day in Dallas. I met a man in prison, Kurt Jager.' Jack leaned over and pulled the knight from his pocket. 'He taught me how to play chess and through the game, how to live a better life.' He held up the chess piece. 'He carved this with a broken piece of glass.'

'My pa played — there's a board somewhere in the house.'

McGraw smiled. 'If you can find it, I'll teach you the game.'

She took the knight from his hand and examined it in minute detail. Her fingers traced its features. 'I'd like that.'

7

Robert Simpson swept dirt from the boardwalk back onto the street. He was a fastidious man who kept his store spotless and his personal appearance neat and tidy. He watched as his son, John, strolled out of the store. He walked past his father and stared up the street at the Timber Saloon.

'Son, I could use your help. The supplies are in from Dallas and need inventoried.'

'Not today, Pa, I got other business to tend to.' He stepped off the boardwalk and crossed the road, heading towards the saloon.

Fear clouded Robert's eyes as he watched his son reposition his rig, slip off the Colt's keeper loop and loosen the holster's grip on his revolver.

'John,' called his father.

If young Simpson heard his father's

call, he ignored it and him. His mind was set on taking Page and his men to task for roughing up Rebecca. They were older, but not any tougher; besides they were busted up, so it should be an easy enough job.

Outside the saloon, John paused at the batwing doors and looked inside to see who was where. He was in luck; Page stood at the bar, and Frank and Billy at their usual table. With a forceful push, he shoved open the swinging doors. They banged against their jambs; everyone jumped and turned to stare. John stood very erect just inside the doors.

'Page, we've got some business to settle.' He circled to his left, so he could keep Billy and Frank in his field of vision.

Three other patrons, who stood at the bar and didn't want to be involved, raised their hands and backed out of the saloon. Page, Frank, and Billy kept their eyes fixed on John's gun hand.

Page leaned back against the bar and

placed his hands on the edge, he hooked his left boot heel on the rail.

'What's put you on the prod, John? I thought we was friends? You know, I've always made sure you got treated right when you was here.'

The bartender moved away from Page and reached beneath the bar.

'Sam,' said John, 'when you stand up, your hands better not be holdin' somethin' that'll put you in an early grave.'

Sam stiffened; slowly, he placed one empty hand, and then the other on the bar top. John nodded, and the bartender moved to the end.

John returned his attention to Page. 'You're done botherin' Rebecca Gottlieb. Any more trouble and I'll consider you the source and come gunnin' for you — understand?'

Page pulled open the lapels of his jacket. 'I'm not armed — '

Frank eased his hand across his cross-draw rig to the butt of his gun, and said, 'That's bold talk for a young pup that ain't shot nothin' but tin cans and empty bottles that don't shoot back.' He sneered, showing his tobacco-stained teeth. 'I kissed your sweetheart.' He spewed a dark stream at the spittoon near his feet. 'She said she liked it, too, and we would've done more if McGraw hadn't stepped in.'

John's eyes squinted to slits; the muscles of his jaw flexed as he tried to control his rising anger. 'If you wasn't busted up, I'd make you eat them words.' He glanced at McCarthy, his grinning face further inflamed John's growing rage. 'That goes for you too, Billy; you're both nothing but snivelling cowards.'

Billy's grin faded and he sat up in his chair.

'That's enough, boys,' said Page. He pushed off the bar and walked over to position himself between John and his men. 'John, there's no need to let this get out of control. Frank and Billy have been taught their lesson.'

John returned his attention to Page. 'You best remember what I said. I'll come for you if Rebecca has any more trouble.'

Page grinned. 'I guess you'll have to stand in line. McGraw made the same promise ahead of you.' Wanting to put his spurs into John, Page added, 'McGraw seems a bit too old for her, but that's the way it is with some women — they like older men.'

John bristled and drew back to swing at Page. Page was quicker; a knife sprang from his sleeve, into his hand and at John's throat in the blink of an eye. John checked his punch, swinging his arms up as he stepped backwards from the blade.

'You've said your piece, John. Maybe you should find somewhere else to buy your liquor.' Page leaned in and removed John's Colt from his holster. 'I'll have Sam bring this over to your daddy's store after you've had a chance to cool down.'

John's face burned red with near uncontrollable anger as Frank and Billy laughed.

'The pup's lost his toy,' said Frank.

Humiliated, John turned and stormed out of the saloon. Sam, who would be the one to face John later, was the only one not smiling as John walked past the bar and out the door.

Clark, back at his desk feeling drowsy from earlier beers, looked up when he heard someone stomping past on the boardwalk. It was John Simpson; head down with a scowled expression. By habit, Clark glanced to John's holster; it was empty.

It didn't take much reasoning to guess what'd happened. Clark sighed, weary of his job, and dreaded the coming confrontation with John Simpson. The young man had a good heart, but he needed to grow up. If he kept on this way, he wasn't going to make it.

The sheriff stood, adjusted his rig, and went after John. When he reached the entrance to Simpson's store, he heard John say, 'I'm not a coward like you — now give it back.' Clark stepped through the door just as Robert

Simpson backhanded his son across the mouth.

John stumbled back, surprise in his eyes. A red blotch formed on his face as blood trickled from his lower lip. Robert's face was dark as he said, 'Don't ever talk to me like that again.'

Clark asked, 'Is there trouble, Robert?'

Robert's head snapped up and he glared at the source of the voice. Seeing that it was the sheriff, he took several deep breathes before speaking. 'Yes, Sheriff, there is. I caught him stealing a gun from my display case and I want him arrested.'

John mustered a protest. 'But, Pa! I work here.'

Robert looked at John. 'I fired you this morning when you wouldn't inventory the supplies — arrest him, Sheriff.'

Clark grinned. 'Yes, sir, Mr Simpson,' he said, emphasizing the mister. He grabbed John's arm and dragged him out.

* * *

81

The cell door clanged as it slammed home.

'Son, you don't know squat about your pa. Thirty years ago, there weren't many people here and those that were had to fight to survive. You ask some of the old-timers about your pa and his courage, when the Alabama-Coushatta and Cherokee were still on the prod.'

'Well, he don't act like it now. Bowin' and scrapin'; yes, sir; no, sir; and my apology, sir.'

Clark shook his head. 'What do you expect? Hell, boy, he runs a business mostly frequented by women. They don't want someone totin' and shootin' iron and talkin' tough, always spoilin' for a fight. He wouldn't be in business no time at all.'

John flopped on to his bunk, not looking at the sheriff. 'Well, I ain't gonna be no dry goods owner.'

'Maybe so,' said Clark. 'Or maybe not. You just sit there and think on it. When you've cooled off, I'll speak to your pa.'

8

Page sat at his desk and stared at Frank and Billy. 'Frank, I ought to kill you. I told you no rough stuff.'

Frank's hand reached for his gun butt, but he checked his move. Something about the look in Page's eyes told him it would be his last, so he let his hand fall away. Page sneered and brought his hands up; he held a .32 Colt Rainmaker in his right.

'So, sometimes you can be smarter than you look,' said Page.

Billy crowded the corner of his chair, trying to put some distance between him and Frank. He'd never seen Page so mad.

'Look, Ben, it was all Frank's doin'. I warned him that you'd have his hide, but he didn't listen.'

Frank glared at Billy. 'You were talkin' rough yourself!'

'It was just to scare her some, I never touched her,' said Billy. He sent a quick glance at Page to see his reaction.

'It's on you, Frank,' said Page. 'You disobeyed my orders and you knew it. So tell me why I shouldn't shoot you? Billy will swear that you pulled that hog-leg.' Page stared at the holstered cap and ball Army Colt, and asked, 'I pay you well enough, why haven't you bought something newer?'

Frank glanced down at his pistol. 'It was my pa's. He claimed it was what kept him alive during the War — that and a bit of luck.'

The tension in the room lessened. Page was still angry, but the danger for Frank had passed. 'How's your leg?' asked Page.

'Doc says it'll be another month afore I can ride, but all I need now is this cane.'

Page nodded and turned to Billy. 'You?'

'Same for me, Ben. Doc says I can shoot again soon enough.'

Page studied them for several seconds. Finally, he said, 'Here's what you're going to do. Billy, get a wagon from the livery and drive the both of you out to the ranch. I don't want to see or hear from you until you're able to ride and shoot.'

Frank grimaced. 'There ain't nothin' to do out there.'

Page smiled. 'That's the point. I don't want you doing anything either there or here in town. Lay low, until all of this blows over. Then we'll make our move.'

9

McGraw scanned the road that ran alongside the field he ploughed; he saw a rider crest the hilltop. He couldn't make out the rider's features, but he recognized the dapple grey pony. It was John Simpson's third Saturday courting Rebecca.

When Simpson came abreast of McGraw, he reined in to survey the farm. 'You've certainly made a change in this place.'

Jack's eyes fell on Simpson's Colt carried in its low-swung, tied down holster. 'It's a good way of life, John, especially if you're plannin' on raisin' a family.'

Simpson glanced at the house and saw Rebecca standing on the porch; her recently ironed dress giving her a crisp, fresh appearance. He looked down at McGraw.

'You don't have to be a farmer.' His tone was disdainful. 'Or a storekeeper to support a family, there're other ways. You wait and see — '

McGraw glanced at Rebecca. 'I don't think she'd agree. Ask her, though, and find out, John. It's plain; she's started to consider you more'n a pretty face.' When Simpson scowled at Jack's comment, he grinned. 'She has a mind of her own — you'll see soon enough.' Simpson looked uncertain. 'Go on, boy, she's waitin' for you. You're all she's talked about today.'

Simpson heeled his pony to a trot towards the house. Rebecca stood erect with her hands behind her back. She smiled and looked at him with her big brown cow's eyes; John's bravado drained away.

'Hello, John, I'm pleased to see you. You're staying for supper?'

He smiled back. 'Wouldn't miss it,' he said as he stepped down from his pony.

He tied the horse's lead to the new

porch post installed since his last visit, and bounded up to the porch and onto its swing. Rebecca sat there, waiting against the backdrop of the newly painted house; the smell of linseed oil hung in the air as the paint cured.

'Mr McGraw killed a deer, so we're having venison for supper.' Her eyes radiated with delight as she stared at him. Her hair fell over her shoulder, and she casually captured a lock and began absently twirling it around her finger. 'I picked some wild berries this morning. I hope you like blueberry pie?'

'Mmm,' he said and rubbed his stomach. In truth, he didn't care for sweets. He ate too many treats at his father's store as a kid, but if Rebecca made it, he'd eat whatever she served.

Lost in each other's company, they paid no attention to McGraw, who'd returned from the field, tended and stabled the animals, and now stood at the foot of the porch.

'Ahem,' he said as he moved up the

steps. They turned with surprised stares. 'I think I'll go inside for some coffee — maybe tend the oven.'

Rebecca jumped up as if stung. 'Oh, I've completely forgotten about the roast.' Panic spread across her red face. 'I hope it's not burnt to a crisp — such a lovely piece of meat.' She hurried through the door. McGraw watched her for a second and then smiled at John before he followed Rebecca.

When he entered, she had the lid off the roasting pan and poked at the venison. 'It's okay, but it needs tending.'

Jack could hear the relief in her voice. He said, 'You go out and sit with your company, or should I say beau. I'll watch this.'

Rebecca's cheeks coloured again, but she didn't protest his words. 'We haven't spoken about that — yet.' She smiled, and the twinkle in her eyes betrayed her coy intentions.

McGraw's laughter was so loud Rebecca shushed him.

'He might hear,' she said as she

glanced over her shoulder at the door.

He quelled his laughter with a hand and turned away. Finally, he turned back, but a grin remained spread across his face.

'I'll make myself scarce after supper. It'll give him a chance to say what's on your mind.' His eyes beamed with laughter.

Rebecca put her hands on her hips and feigned anger. After a few seconds, she relented and smiled. 'I think it's too soon for him to talk about being my beau.'

She ladled two glasses of sweet tea from the crock and hurried to sit with John. She looked back at McGraw and smiled before she went through the door. Outside, she smiled at John.

'The roast is fine. Supper will be ready in an hour or so. Meanwhile, here's some sweet tea.' She held out his glass.

After their supper, McGraw, true to his word, stood with a yawn. 'It's been a long day for me. I hope you young folks will excuse me — I'm turnin' in early. Goodnight, John, hope to see you again real soon.' He turned to Rebecca and winked. In the shadows of the porch, he couldn't see her face, but he was certain that she blushed.

They watched him walk to the barn. A lamp lit, and they could tell from the fluctuating brightness that he moved about his room for several minutes, and then it went black.

'He's done a lot of work out here,' said John, 'more'n you'd expect for just a hired man.'

Rebecca tried to see his face to discover the motive for his comment. Finally, she asked, 'Why do you say that?'

'No reason.'

She drew back and as her expression fell, she said, 'He was raised on a farm. Unlike you soft townies, he knows how to work for a living and most likely takes pride in what he's done.'

John sensed more than heard the hurt in her voice. 'I didn't mean anything, Rebecca. I think it's a wonder what he's done here in a short time, and I'm happy for you. It's just that — '

Rebecca was on him, her tone now fierce, and she asked, 'Just that what?' She'd leaned in, and he could see the set of her jaw as she gritted her teeth.

'Well, he acts like he owns the place, that's all. He ain't your pa, or any other kind of kin. What gives him the right?'

Her eyes stayed fixed on his, finally, she leaned back to her side of the swing. 'John, I believe you're jealous of him. You should be ashamed, he's old enough to be my father.'

John's mouth opened and closed several times as he tried to form a response. He felt his cheeks warming with his embarrassment. Eventually, he said, 'I — I never meant nothin' like that. It's just he acts like he's the one in charge, and you seem to let him. He's the hired man; you're his boss, and you should be tellin' him what to do.'

Her tone softened. 'Maybe he does, but the thing is he knows more about farming than I ever will.' Her tone softened. 'We talk every morning about the day's chores and our long-term plans for the place. I'd be pretty stupid to try and boss him around just because of my pride — or yours.'

He sat quiet for several seconds. 'Rebecca, you talk like you don't want to leave this place.' He paused. 'I — I mean, don't you want to get married and move away?'

Rebecca sat erect and smoothed her dress and crossed her hands in her lap before speaking. 'Are you proposing, John?'

John jumped up like he'd been stabbed with a needle. 'Whoa, Rebecca, I never said nothin' about gettin' hitched.'

She smiled and her eyes laughed at John, but she kept her tone neutral. 'You asked me if I wanted to get married someday. Well, the answer is yes, I do, but to someone who will love this place, the way I do; who will work it and make it prosper.'

He didn't return to the swing. Instead, he parked his backside on the porch railing. Confused, he wondered how the conversation went from Jack McGraw to him proposing. Well, maybe he did want to marry Rebecca someday, but he didn't intend on becoming a sod-buster.

'Listen here, Rebecca — '

'I'm listening, John, what do you have to say?'

'Maybe I do have feelings for you, but I ain't wantin' to become no sod-buster, nor storekeeper either.'

'Then how would you provide for a family?'

'With this,' he said as his hand slipped down to his gun's butt. The leather creaked as he twisted it in its holster. 'I'm good and there are plenty who'd pay for my services.'

Rebecca stopped the swing and sat very still. When she spoke, her tone was heavy with sadness. 'John, I don't think you should come out here ever again.'

'But — '

'I mean it, John. What kind of life

would that be? Always expecting to hear that you're dead? What about the men you'd have to kill? No, I want no part of it, please leave.'

Her words jolted him harder than he would have guessed. He didn't expect her to be so vehemently against his plan to become a hired gunman. Feigning bravado he didn't really feel, he stood to go.

'You'll change your mind, Rebecca, when I'm famous.'

As he descended the step, Rebecca said, 'I couldn't live with that kind of fame. Why is it so important to you?'

He didn't answer. Hurt and angry, John stabbed his boot-toe into the saddle's stirrup, swung up, and galloped away without slowing to look back. As Rebecca watched him depart, her tears transformed into great sobs of anguish.

Unseen, McGraw stood in the shadows of the huge oak tree that shaded the house. He'd snuck from the barn's rear door and hid there listening. The outcome of John's visit was different than he'd expected. He wanted to share in Rebecca's excitement when John declared his intentions. Instead, it was her heartache.

McGraw kept to the shadows and made his way back to the barn. From inside the barn, he jogged across the yard towards Rebecca. 'What's wrong, what happened?'

Surprised by his sudden appearance, she looked up and momentarily checked her sobs. 'How — '

'I heard John light out of 'ere in a hurry. What happened?'

Jack mounted the steps and stood by the swing, unsure if he should sit. He threw caution to the wind and sat beside her.

'Oh, Jack.' She threw herself on to his chest and sobbed, 'I love him so much, but I sent him away. What am I to do? I feel like I'll die if I can't have him.'

It was the first time she'd used his given name. It wasn't Father, but it was better than Mr McGraw. 'Stay here and I'll get you a glass of water. Dry your tears while I'm gone, and then you can tell me all about it. I'm sure we can fix it.'

10

Robert Simpson worked outside his store, wrangling wooden crates filled with tins of saltine crackers. Mrs McKnight, the café owner, would send someone over later to pick them up. He looked up when he heard a horse gallop into town. When he saw who it was, a scowl creased his face; it was his son, John.

Robert knew from the boy's posture and stride that he was angry and looking for trouble. In the Timber Saloon, John was sure to find more than he bargained for. Robert crossed the street, making his way to the saloon. He called, 'John!'

Young Simpson didn't heed his father's call. He pushed through the batwing doors and glared at the few men present who ignored him and returned to minding their own business. Billy McCarthy and Frank were at their usual table outside

Ben Page's office. Things seemed to have quietened down, so Page had called them back to work.

John stormed across the room and stood at their table. 'You two look mended to me, so it's time to face me, or leave town.'

Billy's wrist remained stiff and the idea of shooting a handgun didn't sit well with him. He said, 'Aw, come on, John, what's put a burr under your saddle? It ain't that pretty little farm girl, is it?'

Without warning, John backhanded Billy, knocking him out of his chair. 'When're you goin' to learn not to talk about her?'

Frank, still seated, grabbed the butt of his old Colt; John was faster. He had his Colt drawn and cocked before Frank's hog-leg could clean the leather.

Behind him, just entering the saloon, his father said, 'Don't do it, son. Please, John, I'm begging you not to shoot.'

The blood drained from Frank's face. He released his gun, letting it slide back into its holster as he raised his hands.

'It'd be murder if you shoot now — they'll hang you.'

Billy lay frozen where he landed. The kid was quicker than he thought. Even if his wrist was working, John could beat him on the draw, and he knew it. Deciding discretion was the better part of valour, he said, 'Look, John, I didn't mean anything. I apologize.' Billy stared at Frank's pale face. 'So does Frank — don't you, Frank?'

'Sure, kid, we didn't mean nothin'.' John's glare intensified. 'Come on, kid, we said we was sorry.'

Robert stood directly behind his son. He gently laid a hand on the boy's shoulder. 'Let it go, John.'

John shrugged his father's hand off, leaned forward and stuck the barrel of his Colt under Frank's nose.

'Leave town by tomorrow noon, or I'll kill you on sight.'

From behind the bar with Sam, Ben Page watched the scene unfold. Young

Simpson's speed impressed him, too, but it disappointed him that John didn't kill Frank. He didn't have anything against Frank, but he didn't have a reason to keep him alive either. Ben could use someone with John's fast draw, but he'd have to know that he would kill if need be.

John backed away from Frank and Billy. At the batwing doors, he threw a look at Page. Page nodded and smiled. Robert moved to stand between his son and the men in the room. He protected them as much as he did his son.

'Let's go home, John. Your mother has supper ready, I'm sure.'

Billy climbed up from the floor and dusted himself off. Adrenaline pulsed through his veins and he couldn't stop talking.

'Whew, did you see that? Who knew the kid was so fast? Why, the only thing that saved your life, Frank, is you was so slow — '

'Shut up, Billy, afore I knock you back to the floor.'

Page came to the table. 'What's it going to be, boys? You leavin' town, or shootin' it out with young Simpson?'

'Ah, he was bluffin', wasn't he, Frank?' asked Billy.

'Is that what you think, Frank?' Page gibed the older gunman, the laughter in his eyes plain for all to see.

'He caught me off guard, that's all,' said Frank. He glared at the doors where he'd last seen John. 'I'll be ready the next time we meet.' He absent-mindedly patted the butt of his Colt.

Page glanced at Billy and stared hard at Frank.

'Don't be in here at noon tomorrow. I don't need the trouble. It's your call, boys, either meet him in the street or leave town.'

Billy's eyes grew wide. 'But, boss — '

Coldness from Page's eyes chilled Billy, causing him to recoil. Page said, 'I can't use you boys if what you showed today is the best you got to offer.'

The colour had long returned to Frank's face, and he raged inside at having been made the fool by Simpson. The young fool would pay with his life tomorrow. Frank poked Billy's shoulder.

'Come on, let's get out of here. We got some plannin' to do.'

Frank stood and limped out of the saloon through the back door. Billy followed close behind.

11

Full darkness enveloped the farm. After an hour of consoling Rebecca, she finally retired to her room. McGraw sat on his bunk sipping coffee when he heard a horse ride into the yard. *Was it young Simpson returning to make up with Rebecca?* He stood to investigate. At the barn's door, he met Robert Simpson.

'McGraw, I was afraid you'd be asleep by now.'

Jack cocked his head slightly. It was Simpson's tone; he heard worry and desperation. In a neutral voice, he said, 'Usually are, but Rebecca needed to talk after your boy left.'

'Oh!' Simpson stared blankly at McGraw. It finally dawned on him that John was the source of trouble here, too. His shoulders fell, and his brow rose. 'What did John do?'

Jack raised his hand to quell the anxiety that began to rise in Simpson's voice.

'The boy ain't done nothin' wrong . . . yet. It's just that he has some rash ideas about how to support a family and Rebecca can't accept 'em, so she sent him away. She cried for near an hour.' Simpson began to pace in front of the barn. After several seconds of watching, Jack said, 'You'd best come inside afore you wake her, and she starts at it again.'

Inside Jack's room, he offered Simpson the stool stored beneath the table. From a shelf above his bunk, he took down a bottle of rye and a single glass. He poured a generous portion into the glass, handed it to Simpson, and then splashed a large jigger into his coffee. He looked at Simpson with an empathetic smile.

'Now, suppose you start at the beginning.'

Simpson took a large gulp of the rye and immediately gasped and then coughed several times.

'I don't drink much,' he said by way of an apology. He smiled and consumed a second drink, but smaller this time. A blush came to his cheeks, and he grinned.

With a nod of understanding, Jack said, 'Tell me about it.'

Fortified by the rye, Simpson nodded and began. 'I didn't remember who you were at first, but then the other day when you came to town with Rebecca, it comes to me who you were. It was a shame what happened to you up in Dallas.'

'Why didn't you let on?' asked Jack.

Simpson gave a half-heated shrug. 'It was a long time ago and, well, I guess it was on account of Herman and Dora. They wanted to raise Rebecca as their own and asked for my help. So, I sort of got used to the idea and — '

Jack smiled, reached over and patted Simpson's shoulder. 'I reckon I understand. You get used to thinkin' one way and there don't seem to be no reason to change it, so you don't.'

A relieved expression came to Simpson's face. 'Exactly, besides, you didn't act like you wanted me to say anything.'

'So, why the change?' asked Jack.

Simpson hesitated, and then he plunged forward with why he'd ridden all the way out there. 'It's John. The young fool gave Frank Miller and Billy McCarthy 'til noon tomorrow to leave town, or meet him on the street. They'll kill him, I'm sure. John's never killed anyone.'

Simpson's voice raised an octave, and his eyes pleaded for help. 'I don't think he's ever hurt anything larger'n a fly.'

Stunned, McGraw stared at Simpson for a long time. Finally, he asked, 'Did you tell the sheriff? I mean, what do you expect me to do?'

Simpson knocked back the last of his drink. Jack poured him another. He took a long pull before responding. 'Clark can't do anything until someone is killed.' He quit talking to finish the last of his second drink. Continuing, he added, 'The sheriff thinks Miller is a back shooter and John won't get a fair chance. That's why he suggested I speak with you.'

Jack stared at the storekeeper. He felt very uncomfortable with the pleading expression Simpson displayed. 'Me! What does he think I could do about the situation?'

'You took care of them before and didn't even use a gun. Besides, there's John and your Rebecca. I know if John could just get those fool notions out of his head, he'd be a good match for her.' Simpson's eyes were frantic as he stared at Jack his brow furrowed as if he were in pain. 'Don't you want her to be happy? Mr McGraw, please help me save my son.'

'Mr Simpson, I don't even own a gun.'

McGraw did not refuse outright, which gave Simpson hope, so he pressed on. 'That's not a problem. Take whatever you want from my store. It's yours to keep, just save my boy.'

'Mr McGraw,' called Rebecca, 'is everything all right in there?' She came into the barn carrying her shotgun. The door to McGraw's room stood open, and she started when she recognized Robert Simpson. 'Has something happened to John?' Her free hand flew to her breast, and she bunched her clothing about her neck.

Seeing the blood drain from her face, McGraw stepped to her side to help her remain standing. 'John's just fine, Rebecca, Mr Simpson's here to ask for my help on a personal matter.'

She looked from McGraw, then to Simpson, and then back to McGraw. 'He came out here in the middle of the night?'

With a sheepish grin, he shrugged. 'Like I said, it's personal and he wanted my help right away — ain't that right, Simpson?'

'Rebecca, I need your father's help to save John!'

Only three words of what he said registered: father, save, and John. Her eyes grew very big as she realized the ramifications of Simpson's words. She looked at McGraw's face, studying his features as though searching for something she couldn't explain.

'Mr Simpson called you my father. Why?'

Jack looked at Simpson pleadingly, but it was obvious that he would not rescind his words. McGraw deflated and dropped on to his bunk and stared up at Rebecca. 'It's very complicated,' he said.

She sat on the bed next to him. 'Tell me — '

Including the time spent dealing with her questions, it took the better part of an hour to explain everything fully. When they finished, she asked, 'Who else knows?'

Simpson stared up at nothing as he considered. 'Your father — I mean grandfather — kept family matters close. I don't think most folks knew Rebecca, your mother, was even pregnant. When your father got sent away

110

only the telegraph operator knew, and he's been replaced twice since.' He halted, rubbing the unaccustomed stubble on his chin. 'Of course there's Doc Benson, but he'd never betray a confidence. So I guess that leaves me, maybe a few others if you were to remind them. Why?'

She turned to McGraw who'd been watching her every reaction. 'Were you ever going to tell me?'

'I hoped I'd be able to someday. It's just that — '

'What did my mother look like? Are there any pictures of my mother? Why did they keep all this from me?' Her tone grew angrier with each question. She threw herself into Jack's arms and began to cry. Simpson looked on impatiently.

McGraw reached over and took the broken mirror he'd brought inside from the wash station and held it up for Rebecca to see. 'This is what your mother looked like, she was beautiful.'

Rebecca looked at her reflection and saw her red runny nose and puffy eyes.

She half-heartedly laughed and pushing his arm away, she said, 'Not like that, she wasn't.'

'She was always beautiful to me and so are you.'

She stopped her sniffles, and blew her nose. McGraw removed the shotgun from her lap before it fell to the floor. 'What do we do about John, Father? What's the trouble he's in?'

Her tone said she'd accepted who he was. He couldn't help but smile like an expectant father. 'I don't know, Becca.' He grinned at getting to use the pet name once again. 'John has called out Frank Miller and Billy McCarthy. The sheriff can't do anything 'til someone's shot or killed. He sent Mr Simpson out here to get my help.'

'But can you help him, Father?'

McGraw patted her hands as they clung to his arm. 'We'll do what we can.' He looked up at Simpson, whose expression shone relief for the first time since his arrival. He turned back to his daughter. 'Becca, do you think you

could convince John to go riding,'
McGraw opened his watch case, 'this
morning?'

12

Frank Miller and Billy McCarthy sat by their campfire and nursed their bottle of rye.

'It ain't fair we gotta be out here,' said Billy, as he pulled a blanket around his shoulders.

'We'll take care of Simpson tomorrow, and then things'll be like they were. I'm goin' to truly enjoy seein' him get it.'

'I don't know, Frank. The kid is pretty darn fast — faster'n me leastwise. Maybe we should give it up and move on.'

'What fer, we got a good setup here. Besides, my leg — '

'It ain't worth gettin' killed for. Let's get while we can.'

A sinister scowl fell across Frank's face as he jerked the bottle from Billy and took a long pull. He nearly emptied the bottle.

'Hey, don't drink it all,' protested Billy as he jerked back the bottle. Billy held it up to the light to examine its content. He glared at Frank, and then put the bottle to his lips and tilted his head back. The rye burned his throat.

As Billy finished the bottle, Frank pulled his hog-leg and let go a round, shattering the bottle above Billy's face. Shards flew; a couple drew blood.

Billy bolted upright and fumbled for his Colt. Frank pointed his iron at his partner. 'Take it easy. I got a plan.'

With no other choice, Billy released his gun and settled back. 'Why'd you shoot the bottle?' He pressed a dirty bandanna against a scalp wound to stop the blood trickling into his eye.

'It's part of my plan. Here's what we're goin' to do.'

★   ★   ★

Though dressed like a boy, there was no denying that Rebecca was a woman. She halted in front of Simpson's store.

The store was closed, so she heeled McGraw's dun around, past the side of the store to the residence around the back. It was a small, four-room house painted white with a matching picket fence. Sarah Simpson's flower garden was in full bloom, displaying colours that only nature could create. Rebecca paused for only an instant to admire the flora and their smells before dismounting.

Robert Simpson, who expected her arrival, sat on the porch drinking coffee. His wife and John were still in the kitchen.

'Good morning, Rebecca, this is a pleasant surprise.' He winked.

'And to you, Mr Simpson. Is John home?'

Simpson stepped to the door and called, 'John, you have a visitor — a very pretty one at that.' He turned back and smiled at Rebecca, who blushed, and again he winked.

John came through the door; his hair was mussed, and he was tucking in his shirttail. He smiled, and his eyes lit up when he saw Rebecca.

'John, I've come to apologize. Will you go riding with me?' She stared at him with glistening brown eyes and bit at her lower lip. Barely audible, she added, 'Please.'

Caught off guard, John hesitated, but seeing her expression, he couldn't refuse her. 'Sure, that'd be swell, but just for a while, I got business to deal with later this morning.'

He jumped from the porch. The dun stepped away, and he grabbed its bridle to settle her. He noticed Rebecca's trousers.

'When'd you start dressin' like a boy?'

She teased him with her smile and lifted a single brow. 'Only when I go riding, do you disapprove?' she asked.

'My horse is at the livery, I'll be right back.'

She watched him jog away. After he turned the corner of the store, she looked at Mr Simpson.

'Father — ' She paused. It pleased

her to call Jack that. Rebecca knew Herman loved her, but there was always something missing; a grandfather's love is not the same as a father's. Looking back, she'd felt something the first day Jack McGraw rode on to the farm. 'Father will ride in once we've left. He'll come straight to your house.'

Simpson nodded. 'I'll be waitin'.' He looked at her curiously. 'You sure you can keep him away 'til past noon?'

This time it was her turn to wink. 'One way or another — '

John's quick return surprised them, and they stopped talking as he trotted to the house. 'You ready?'

Mr Simpson smiled at his son. 'You never move that quickly when I ask.' He turned to Rebecca. 'Maybe you can at that.'

John glanced at his father, and then to Rebecca. He tilted his head slightly and started to ask, but then said nothing.

Sarah Simpson came out in time to see them off. As they rode away, she commented, 'They make such a pretty couple. If only John would give up his dangerous notions and settle down.'

Minutes later, McGraw reined in and swung down from his mule. Leaving Sarah, Simpson nodded and stepped from the porch and led the way to his store's rear entrance. Sarah watched them go; her face held a perplexed expression, but she asked nothing.

Inside the store, Simpson led McGraw to the gun case. 'Take whatever you want. I've plenty of cartridges, and holsters are over there.' He pointed to the saddle section of the store.

Jack shook his head. 'I've watched the town since sunup. I saw McCarthy climb into the church's steeple with his carbine. It was before folks were up and about. Miller is waitin' at the Timber. When John shows to fight it out, Billy will get him.'

'What a' you gonna do?'

McGraw moved to the store's hardware section. When he found a barrel of wooden tool handles, he rummaged

119

through the offering. At length, Jack selected an axe handle made of hickory. As he repeatedly slapped the business end into the palm of his hand, he said, 'I was hopin' you could prevail on Sheriff Clark to keep an eye on Billy, while I talk things over with Miller.'

Simpson nodded; his eyes were dark, and a knife cut formed his mouth. 'I'll get him now,' he said, and moved for the door.

McGraw called after him, 'I'll give you forty-five minutes to get set. Come back if you can't find him in time.'

Simpson left through the back, McGraw followed. Sarah Simpson was still on the porch. She stared after her husband, who'd disappeared at a trot around the corner two buildings down directly across from the sheriff's office.

As McGraw approached the house, Sarah smiled nervously. She repeatedly tugged the red chequered kitchen towel's edges through her hands, and asked, 'Will you please tell me what's happening? I know this has something to do with John, but Robert says to be patient and that everything's fine.'

The pleading in her eyes and worry in her voice compelled him to speak. 'John has done something foolish and dangerous. Rebecca, Robert, and I are trying to prevent his getting hurt.'

Tears began to well in her fear-widened eyes. 'Please tell me. What has John done that has you and Robert so concerned?'

McGraw stared at her, trying to decide what he should do. Finally, he sighed, and said, 'He's called out two men, Frank Miller and Billy McCarthy for noon today.'

Sarah paled and brought her hands to her mouth as she gasped.

'You can't be serious.' But she knew that he was and her knees felt weak. She grabbed the porch's rail to keep from falling.

McGraw saw her stumble, and he bounded up the steps and grabbed her elbow and guided her to a chair. 'You should sit.'

She did as McGraw instructed. From her chair, she studied McGraw's face for several seconds. 'Please don't think me ungrateful, but why would you, a complete stranger, get involved? I mean, you hardly know us.'

'I know you better'n you think. 'Sides, Rebecca's in love with John and she wants him kept safe.'

Sarah's eyes glanced down to watch McGraw fondle a carved object. 'What is that you're doing, Mr McGraw?' she asked.

Jack looked down, he wasn't aware that he'd taken the knight from his pocket. He smiled half-heartedly at Sarah.

'Decidin' my next move.' He held up the chess piece and studied its features. 'I have several choices, but only one will win the day.'

Robert returned the way he came. 'I've found Clark and he's in place. I told him you weren't going to carry a gun when you brace Miller, and he says you're stupid or crazy, maybe both.'

McGraw returned the knight to his pocket and brought out his timepiece. He flipped the lid open to check the time, but his stare was drawn to the portrait of Rebecca's mother made at about Rebecca's age now. They look so alike, he thought. It was nearly eight o'clock; he closed the lid and said, 'It's time.'

* * *

The dun was half a hand taller than John's pony, and with her lighter weight, Rebecca easily pulled ahead as they raced to the stand of willow trees near the stream. She reined to a halt and hopped down; she laughed with her delight at winning the race. John was right behind her. Both smiled, as they walked their horses to the water and allowed them to drink.

John tied the horses' leads to a nearby sapling, so they could graze on the tender grasses on the stream's banks. Though it was morning, the sun's rays warmed the air. Rebecca untied the blanket roll from behind her saddle and ducked under a willow tree's canopy and spread it out to enjoy the cool shade.

With a toss of his hat, John joined her. As he dropped to his knees, he unbuckled his gun and holster, and laid it alongside his hat. Rebecca watched; her normally large eyes were slits as they followed the Colt's movement like a prairie dog watches a rattlesnake as it slithers near their den.

Noticing her stare, John placed his hat over the gun. Rebecca's eyes looked up into his. They were wide once again; she searched his as she wetted her lips.

Colour rushed to John's face as his heartbeat increased. He leaned forward, hesitated only a second, and then kissed Rebecca on the mouth. She kissed him back, pulling him down on to her.

John reared up, his breathing fast, his cheeks heated; he looked down on her with questioning eyes. 'We should stop.'

Rebecca smiled, but her eyes were

laughing as she said, 'If you think it best. I wouldn't want you to think badly of me.'

John pulled free of her embrace and sat next to her, staring at the water; his posture unyielding. 'That's not what I meant. It's just that I'm a man and if things should go too far, well — '

She put her hand on his arm, and he turned to look at her. The watery stare of her eyes weakened his resolve. 'I would be lying if I said I didn't want you, but you're right. We should wait until we're married.'

John stiffened again. 'Rebecca,' his tone was pleading, 'I told you I wasn't cut out to be a sod-buster or a storekeeper.'

She sat up, hugging his arm to her. 'I understand that you're not ready right now, but soon. I'm willing to wait.'

It wasn't exactly what he wanted to hear, but it would do for now. He leaned against the willow tree and Rebecca curled up under his arm. John fished out his watch, but before he opened the case, Rebecca said, 'We've plenty of time before noon.'

John looked down at her. 'What makes you say that?'

Rebecca uncurled herself. Ignoring him, she went to her horse and rummaged in her saddle-bags. 'I've brought sandwiches and two bottles of sarsaparilla. Put them in the creek to cool, please.'

He took the bottles of reddish-brown liquid from her and placed them on the sandy creek bed. The water was cold and made his wrist hurt.

'They'll be cool soon enough, I reckon.' He rubbed his hands together for warmth.

Under the tree, Rebecca spread out a red and white chequered table cloth. In the centre, she placed sandwiches in folded napkins and two canned jars; sweet pickles and peaches. She smiled at him. 'I hope you're hungry.'

He unfolded one of the white napkins. Between two slices of three-quarter-inch buttered bread, he found a fried egg and bacon filling. He smiled at her. 'Always.'

Halfway through their sandwiches, John retrieved the drinks from the creek. He used a corner of the tablecloth to dry them, and he opened them, handing her the one he thought coldest.

They finished their picnic without further conversation. As he helped her gather things up, he asked again, 'Why did you mention noon?' His stare didn't allow her to ignore him again.

She saw that she couldn't put him off any longer. 'Your father came out to our farm last night.'

By John's expression, she could see his confusion. He asked, 'Why did my father come out there to see you?'

'He didn't. He came out to see my father.'

John studied her face to see if she were putting him on, but saw only a matter-of-fact stare. 'Your father?' he asked.

She smiled. 'It's a bit complicated.

You see, John McGraw is my father.' Herman and Dora were my mother's parents and they raised me as their own, so I'd never known about my father.'

John dropped back on to the table-cloth. 'Well, that explains his attitude, I guess.' He paused to think about what she'd said. 'So, that was why my father came out there? But that doesn't make any sense at all.' He paused again. 'You said he came out to see Jack, your father. What for?'

'He figured my father could keep you from getting killed today at noon.' Her lips now formed a colourless slit, and her pinched brow created deep furrows. Had she stood, her hands would be firmly placed on her hips. Her voice rose to match her level of concern and anger. 'My father agreed to help because he knows I don't want you to get hurt, or worse.'

John snatched his watch from his pocket and released the lid; 10.30. He had an hour and a half to get back to town. 'Rebecca, let's go. If we leave now we'll be back in plenty of time.'

Rebecca crossed her arms and leaned against the willow's trunk. 'I'm not ready to leave, and you can't make me.'

The quandary gave him pause; his jaw muscles flexed, and he glared at her angrily, but she just smiled at him. The amusement in her eye only served to fuel his frustration. Finally, he said, 'You're right — I can't make you go, but you can't keep me here, either.' He stood, crammed his hat on his head, and then grabbed his rig. In a practised order, he buckled the gun belt, situated its position, tied the rawhide strap around his leg, drew the Colt, and opened the cylinder's gate to check the bullets. Finished, he returned it to his holster, slipped the keeper loop over the hammer tang, and tugged it taut.

'You would ride off and leave me here unprotected?'

He smiled at her feigned worry. 'You rode into town alone. I 'spect you can do it again.'

'But I don't know the way. I wasn't paying attention.' This time there was real worry in her voice.

John believed her this time. 'Then gather your things and come with me.' She made no effort to move. 'All right, the road is a half-mile in that direction.' He pointed. 'Head east when you reach it — it's a straight shot from there.'

He mounted and rode away from the creek, and then reined in and looked back at Rebecca. She hadn't moved. 'If that's the way you want it, then so be it. I'm goin' back to town, I'm leavin'.' She turned her head.

With a great sigh, he said, 'Women!' and heeled his pony into a ground-eating gallop towards town.

Clark was out of sight from Frank Miller, but he could see the church steeple. If Billy McCarthy popped up with a rifle, he'd be the one surprised.

McGraw walked behind the buildings until he was abreast of the Timber Saloon. From the alley way, he could see Frank Miller sitting in a chair in front of the saloon. It was still early and the townsfolk were not milling about yet.

With the axe handle at his side, McGraw stepped out into view and crossed the street. Miller reacted the second he saw a man come out of the shadows. He rocked his chair forward as he grabbed for the handle of his hog-leg Colt. Miller squinted; recognizing McGraw, he released his gun and returned his chair against the saloon's wall.

'Thought you was the Simpson boy.'

'And if I was?' McGraw asked as he continued across the road.

Miller smirked. 'You'd be dead is what — '

A shot rang out around the corner of the building. Miller and McGraw turned to stare at the church steeple. Billy McCarthy stood with his hands in the air.

'That'd be Clark. He's got the drop on Billy. I ought to let you face John Simpson, but he's not a killer and I don't want him to start now.'

Miller stared at McGraw as if he spoke Mandarin Chinese. Then understanding shone in his eyes, but it was too late. McGraw was on him; he bolted up the three steps. Before Miller could rock his chair forward, McGraw hooked the toe of his boot under a leg and kicked up. Miller's arms flew out as he tried to check the fall. Trapped in his chair, Miller stared up at McGraw who had the axe handle propped on his shoulder. Jack's face was impassive.

'Go for that iron and I'll crack your skull.'

'That'd be murder and you'd go back to prison.'

Miller saw just a flicker of hesitation in Jack's eyes and grabbed for his Colt. As McGraw brought down the axe handle across Miller's arm, the sound of bones cracking was sickening.

'Maybe you're right, but I don't think the sheriff will bother with just a broken arm. You got an hour to get Doc to set that arm and get out of town.' He reached down and retrieved Miller's Colt. 'You can pick this up at Clark's office on your way out of town.' McGraw turned to leave, but stopped. 'I ever see you again, I'll put three slugs into your chest — believe me?'

Miller nodded with a sneer, and said, 'You'll never see me.'

McGraw understood his meaning. 'If you try, don't miss.'

Clark came around the corner behind Billy McCarthy, whose hands were still in the air. 'What do you want to do with them, McGraw? I'm pretty sure I can come up with somethin'.'

Jack smiled. 'Let Billy get Frank over to the doc's. They're leavin'; don't 'spect we'll be seein' 'em again.'

Clark prodded Billy with his rifle barrel. 'You heard him — get your friend over to Doc's and be gone after he's fixed up.'

Billy nodded and climbed on to the porch to help Miller.

Clark and McGraw watched them walk towards Doc Benson's office.

'McGraw, that was a foolhardy stunt, goin' against Miller with just an axe handle. I'm surprised you ain't dead.'

A huge grin spread across McGraw's face. 'Look at it this way; you don't have to arrest me for shootin' 'im. They'll be gone shortly, and young Simpson still has a chance to grow up.'

It was near 11.30 when Clark and McGraw saw John Simpson galloping into town. At Clark's wave, John reined in his pony. He threw a stern glance at McGraw, who smiled in return. He turned to Clark.

'What is it, Sheriff? I have business waitin'.'

Clark stepped out on to the street and held the bridle of John's horse. 'It's all over, John. They've left town.'

John reacted as if he'd been struck in the face. 'I don't believe it. Both of 'em left town without a fight?'

'I wouldn't say that,' said Clark, his words followed with a grin. 'McGraw there saved your life. You should be grateful.'

With restrained anger, John said, 'Mr McGraw, Rebecca told me about you bein' her pa, and I'm happy for her, but you need to stay out of my business. I know what I'm doin'.'

'Is that so?' said Clark. His tone carried rebuke. 'You didn't have a chance. McCarthy was waitin' in the church steeple and when you pulled on Miller . . . ' He stopped and shook his head. 'Son, you're a damn fool. A lot of people are tryin' to help you. I just hope you live long enough to see it for yourself.'

John's bravado faded. 'I — I didn't think about an ambush.'

McGraw stepped to the boardwalk's edge. 'Where's Rebecca?'

'She's fine. She wouldn't leave with me, so I left her by the creek. Rebecca can take care of herself.'

'I'll get my horse. I want you to show me where you left her,' said McGraw. 'She knows the way between the farm and town, but elsewhere is a different story.'

John's face blanched. 'She should have come with me.'

'No!' said McGraw, his anger rising. 'You should have stayed with her. If anythin' happens to her, you'll answer to me.'

Suddenly, John felt like a little boy who'd taken on more than he could handle and now someone else may be in danger.

'Please hurry, Mr McGraw.'

Jack ran to Simpson's house. Robert and Sarah came out of the house to greet him.

'Sorry, I can't talk. John is fine — talk to Clark.' With that said, he was in the saddle, riding for Main Street and John Simpson.

13

Billy led Miller's horse as they rode out of town. Doc Benson gave Frank a generous dose of laudanum, so staying on his saddle was all Frank could manage. They were three or four miles out of town, when Billy noticed a dust cloud headed their way. Given the results of their morning, he was cautious, so he reined the horses into a stand of trees several yards off the trail.

He grimaced when he saw it was John Simpson riding hell-bent for Crockett. A sudden impulse rushed over him to steal a shot from ambush but then, what if he missed? Billy checked the urge and waited for Simpson, and the churning dust cloud that followed, to crest the rise before he led Miller back to the trail.

As they returned to the road, picking their way through tall grass, Billy halted when he saw another rider coming from the same direction Simpson had. He hesitated; the rider was smaller of stature and rode with less urgency. Something about the horseman intrigued him, so he held his ground and waited.

As the rider closed, he recognized Rebecca Gottlieb and his face flushed with unreasoning anger. There she was . . . the source of all their trouble. Without further thought, his rage prevailed, and he dropped the lead for Miller's horse and bolted on to the road, blocking her passage.

Rebecca's horse skidded to a halt, and then reared, clawing the air with its hoofs; she fell to the ground. She landed on her back, knocking the wind from her lungs, which left her momentarily stunned. Billy jumped down and before she could rally for a fight, he tied her hands and feet.

She struggled to a seated position. 'What do you think you're doing, Billy?' She glanced over and saw Miller with a bandaged arm in a sling. 'They'll hang you two for this.' The sneer on his lips and the malice in his eyes scared her. 'Let me go and I won't say a word, I promise. I'll tell them my horse threw me.'

'I don't think so. It's your fault we got to run out of town.'

Her eyes widened with concern. 'My fath — ' She quickly tried to recover from her mistake. 'I mean, Mr McGraw is not hurt?'

Billy stared at her for several seconds. 'McGraw used to talk about his daughter in prison. He was always goin' on about how he would make it up to her. So, Jack McGraw is your long-lost father.' He began to laugh. 'This is perfect. McGraw will get his due now.' Rebecca started to struggle against the ropes. 'It ain't no use, Miss McGraw.' Like a snake, he hissed the Miss. 'Them knots won't come loose.'

When he stood her up, she continued to struggle. Finally, Billy cuffed her on the jaw. Dazed, she swayed, nearly falling but Billy caught her and heaved her across the dun's saddle.

'When you decide to stop fightin', you can fork that horse proper like.' He set off at a trot and held that pace for ten minutes, bouncing her midsection against the saddle.

'I'll cooperate, please let me sit upright.' Billy halted their horses and dragged Rebecca off the saddle. She was dizzy from the experience, so she responsibly sat on her butt. It wasn't at all dignified; she was grateful to be wearing trousers.

Dismounting, Billy stood over her and drew his knife. For just a split second, fear flashed in her eyes. It was what he wanted to see; he smirked and then cut the rope from her ankles. She was too weak to struggle, or even to assist with mounting. Billy hefted her on to the saddle and tied her hands to its horn.

They were headed for Arkansas where Billy had family and friends who would hide them while Miller's arm mended.

John led McGraw straight to the willow tree. Trampled grass and hoof prints gave ample evidence of their picnic. McGraw dismounted to inspect the tracks in and out of the site. The dun's gait was longer than their horses, and when he examined them closely, he saw that a nail from its right hind shoe worked loose. It was a tiny mark, but once he knew what to watch for, tracking Rebecca wouldn't be a problem if he found her soon.

'She rode out of here headed for the main road,' said McGraw as he remounted his horse and led off at a gallop.

At the main road, McGraw halted and dismounted to scan the ground's offerings at a closer view. He saw where she turned back towards town; he hoped they'd somehow missed her, and she was at Simpson's house or store. Jack was about to remount, when he saw the dun's tracks headed the other way. He walked several yards eastward, inspecting the shoe prints. The dun was one of three horses headed east.

Jack's stomach clenched; he squeezed his calloused hands into white-knuckled fists, and looked at John. 'She's been taken.'

'What!' said John, who stared at McGraw for several moments, his face blanched and fear and worry shone in his eyes. He refused to believe what he'd heard. 'How can that be?'

'Did you see anyone on the road when you returned to town?'

'No one — ' John paused to consider. 'But I was riding fast; I guess someone could've been hidin' along the trail.'

The tracks were fresh and easy to read.

'Let's backtrack a bit and see what we can find out,' said Jack as he mounted.

'But maybe we can catch them?' said John, looking eastward.

'And maybe not.' Jack was fondling the chess piece. 'We'll backtrack and learn all that we can. We need to understand what happened to devise a plan of action. Running off half-cocked could get her, or us killed, then what?'

John's shoulders slumped; he laid the reins across his horse's neck, and they headed back towards Crockett. A few miles of slow riding paid off with dividends, they came across the site where Billy had captured Rebecca. On the ground, both John and Jack searched for clues.

'Here,' said John, following tracks that led to a stand of trees. 'They must've hid in there.' He pointed.

Jack worried the knight between his fingers; he stared eastward with a furrowed brow. He turned to John; clarity shined bright in his eyes. 'McCarthy and Miller took her. They were headed east when they left town, saw you comin' and hid. Once you passed, they saw Rebecca trailin', and they snatched her.'

'You should have stayed out of it,' said John, anger heavy in his voice. 'I'd have killed them and Rebecca would be safe.'

'Weren't you listenin' to Clark? You'd be dead now, and Rebecca heartbroken. I don't know what she sees in you, boy, but she wants you alive, and I promised her I'd keep you that way.'

'Either way, she'd be safe.' John brooded. 'So, now what?'

McGraw climbed back on his horse. 'You're goin' back — '

'I'm comin' with you; ain't no way you can stop me.'

Jack hung his head and took several breaths. 'Let me finish. You're goin' back to Crockett to alert the sheriff, so he can get a posse formed. Then go to your pa's store. There's a Colt .45 Peacemaker on the far end of the gun case. Get it and put together a rig with plenty of ammo. There's a .50 long rifle — get that, too. Don't wait for Clark, you head straight back here. I'll leave signs for you to follow.' He paused to consider. 'I figure you'll catch up to me in about four hours.'

144

* ★ ★

Almost to the minute, four hours later, John rode up the trail. He led a pack horse with supplies and two fresh horses. As John reined in the horses, Jack dismounted and loosened his saddle.

'Good thinkin' to bring extra horses. It'll help us catch up sooner.' He looked towards the eastern sky. 'I hope it don't rain. If we get a break with the weather, we could catch 'em afore they get out of Texas.'

John turned a worried gaze to the clouds forming in the far distant sky. 'It'll hold off, it just has to.'

Jack buckled on the gun rig, mounted while holding the long rifle, which he nestled across his legs. After he was settled, John passed him a piece of jerky.

'Thanks,' said Jack, 'I was getting hungry, but I didn't want to stop 'til we had to.'

For the first hour or so, they didn't

145

speak. McGraw kept his eyes glued to the ground, watching for the slightest change. His tracking abilities were maximized but if it rained, he was at a loss as to what they'd do then. He estimated McCarthy and Miller started with a four hour lead, which because of Jack and John's slow pace, stretched out to a full day.

'I figure they got a day's lead. We'll ride as late as we dare and be at it again at first light. McCarthy has family, and I reckon friends, in Arkansas. There's a fork in the road ahead; we'll see it tomorrow. If they go left, it's Arkansas they're headed for. We can pick up the pace least-ways as far as Nacogdoches. Miller ain't goin' to be no help, and they'll have to be careful near towns. Havin' to keep Rebecca tied is a problem for 'em. It just may help us catch up.'

'What do you figure their plans for Rebecca are?' asked John with concern that became ever present in his voice.

Jack glanced at John. He saw the

worry on the boy's face, but he didn't see how sugarcoating the situation would help.

'It's hard to tell, John. With McCarthy it's more about gettin' even with me. I think he'll tire of havin' her underfoot after a while. There're places in Louisiana where young white girls will bring a high price, but Miller would say no to that.'

John said, 'But you said he's got a busted arm.'

'That he does. He won't try anything with her while he's hurt. She's sure to use that against him if he did.' Jack saw John's shoulders relax. 'Our best chance is to catch up afore they get into Louisiana.' Full darkness fell while they talked. 'I hear water. There must be a stream close. Let's make camp.'

★ ★ ★

The laudanum was gone and the throbbing in Miller's arm grated on his nerves. 'Damn it, Billy, I need to hole up 'til my arm stops hurtin' so bad.'

'You shouldn't have used up the laudanum so fast. Doc Benson said it should last a week.'

'Yeah, but he ain't ridin' a stiff-legged horse that's jolting my bones with every step. Come on, Billy . . . '

Billy looked at Miller and the horse he rode. 'Why don't you ride the dun? She seems like a gentler ride.'

The idea perked up Miller's attitude. 'That's a good idea; I should have thought of it. It's near dark; let's stop for today, and I'll start out fresh on the dun tomorrow.'

They rode off the trail into a clearing that, judged by its appearance, had been used by many travellers before them. A fire ring of burnt stones located the campsite's centre. Some long-ago individuals had dragged a couple of fair-sized logs to use as seats, or windbreaks on blustery nights. There were enough standing trees to break up any rising smoke, so long as the wood was dry.

Billy helped Miller down, unsaddled his horse and made him reasonably comfortable resting on his bedroll and saddle. He untied and pulled Rebecca down from the dun.

'Start gatherin' wood for a fire. Frank, watch her while I tend the horses.'

Miller wrestled his hog-leg Colt from its holster with his left hand. 'I ain't the best shot with my left, but from here I can't miss, so don't get no ideas about runnin' off.'

Rebecca rubbed her wrists to promote blood circulation and looked around the site. Miller watched her closely as she walked about, bending to pick up small limbs and cradle them in her arm. As she worked, Rebecca erred too close to Miller. He was ready; he'd laid his pistol down close beside him and waited.

Miller reached out and grabbed her ankle, and tried to drag her closer. Rebecca dropped most of the firewood, save one club-sized log. She whirled and swung the log down on Miller's broken arm. He let go of her leg to comfort his arm, and in doing so exposed the Colt tucked under his side.

Rebecca saw it, and she dove at it to get it away from Miller. As she came up on her knees holding the pistol and fumbling with the hammer, darkness suddenly fell.

Billy was near when Miller grabbed Rebecca. He'd arrived in time to slam his pistol barrel against the back of her head. She uttered a slight whimper and fell over unconscious.

'You fool,' said Billy, 'she'd have killed you if I hadn't been close by.'

'Did you kill her?' Miller actually sounded concerned.

Billy examined her. 'Nah, but she won't be fixin' vittles.' He dragged her over to her bedroll and covered her with a blanket. 'Damn it, Frank. Now I got two of you to deal with.'

'It weren't my fault. She was tryin' to brain me and escape.'

McCarthy shook his head; disgust with his partner shone plain on his face.

'I saw what you did, Frank. I ought to ride out and leave the two of you to fend for yourselves.'

'Don't be that way, Billy. She'll be fine, you just wait.'

When morning came, McCarthy rose and added wood to the hot coal to start a new blaze for coffee and breakfast. He stared down on Rebecca. She hadn't moved. He lifted one of her eyelids and the eye below was glazed and unfocused. Her breathing was shallow and her colour pale. Billy McCarthy didn't think she'd live past the day. Angry, he walked over and kicked Miller awake.

'She's the same as dead; you caused me to kill a woman.'

Miller flinched from the pain to his arm, and he glared at Billy. Finally, the meaning of his words registered, and Frank's eyes shot to Rebecca's unchanged form lying on the ground.

'You didn't mean to — you was savin' my life. It was an accident.'

'If you'd left her alone, she'd still be alive.'

'Whoa, Billy, you said we brought her along for our enjoyment. What else was you thinkin' to do with her?'

'I ain't thought about it. We shouldn't have snatched her in the first place. McGraw's goin' to be after us sure. I know him from prison. Once he finds out his daughter's been murdered, he won't give up hunting us 'til we're dead.'

Miller's expression brightened. 'Hey, we can use that to our advantage. We'll set up an ambush and kill the sum-bitch.'

Billy stared at Miller. 'Don't you mean I'll set up the ambush, and I'll be the one to backshoot him?'

'Aw, Billy, you know I can't do nothin' with this arm.' He used his good arm to gesture to the broken one.

Billy's eyes hardened, which caused Miller to shrink back. 'You're goin' to be part of the ambush all right — you're goin' to be part of the bait.' He went to the fire and stoked it to a larger flame, and then added a few pieces of damp wood, causing a flume of white smoke to rise above the tree line. 'You're goin' to lie next to Rebecca real friendly like. When he sees you, he'll rush in, and then I get 'im.'

Miller worked his way up to his knees. 'That's crazy, Billy. Why, I'd be out in the open with a crippled arm, unable to shoot.'

McCarthy sneered at his partner. 'It's your choice; if you don't, I'm leavin' to let you deal with 'im alone.'

Late in the afternoon, John saw smoke drifting above the tree tops.

'Look, someone's made camp,' said John. 'Maybe they've seen Rebecca.' John heeled his pony before Jack could stop him.

'Wait.'

John didn't hear, and he rode straight for the smoke. He slowed as he neared the clearing. He saw two figures on the ground; they appeared to be sleeping. One was a smaller figure, and then he saw her face; it was Rebecca.

'Rebecca,' John called.

He dropped off his horse, running as it slid to a halt. The blanket flew back and Frank Miller squirmed to get his left arm up for a shot. The movement caught John's attention and he immediately recognized Miller. The outlaw jerked the Colt hog-leg up, cocking the hammer as it rose.

John dropped to one knee, pulling his own revolver as Miller fired. His shot went wide. John's hand was steady and his aim accurate. He put two successive slugs in the centre of Miller's chest.

Miller hunched around the wounds, and rolled away from Rebecca. He spoke his last words. 'I only kissed her.'

Branches broke in the nearby trees, and then, John heard a horse gallop away. Behind him, Jack McGraw's horse came to a sliding halt and Jack jumped down to examine Rebecca. John already had her in his arms.

'Is she alive?' asked Jack.

John looked up bewildered. 'Yes, but she's been hurt.'

Now on his knees beside them, Jack

gently touched Rebecca's throat, feeling for a pulse. 'It's weak but steady.' The dried blood in her hair guided them to her skull injury. 'John, put her on her side, so I can tend to her scalp wound.'

Jack rushed to his saddle and brought back water and bandages. Tenderly, Jack cleaned the gash over her right ear and bound her scalp.

'Make her comfortable, John, while I set up camp. We can't move her 'til she's awake.' Tears welled in his eyes, and his voice trembled as he added, 'I pray to God she does.' He busied himself, leaving John to hold Rebecca.

Jack dragged Miller's body off into the trees downwind of camp so the horses wouldn't be skittish. When he returned, he saw that John had wrapped Rebecca in a blanket and laid her against her saddle. A coffee pot simmered, and the aroma brought a sense of comfort to Jack. A cup of hot coffee seemed to do more to calm him than the best whiskey that had passed his lips.

'Put some jerky on to boil. It'll make a good broth for when she wakes. She may be a woman, but she's young and has a strong appetite.' Jack led the horses. 'I'll tend to the animals and while I'm down by the stream, I'll see if there's trout.'

A little digging with his knife produced worms for bait, and twenty minutes later, Jack pan-fried the trout. The smell of fish cooking mixed with wood burning wafted across the camp in the afternoon's soft breeze.

Rebecca stirred and let out gentle moans. John emptied his coffee cup with a toss and rushed to her side. He lifted and cradled her in his lap. 'Rebecca, can you hear me?'

Her eyes fluttered open and widened with surprise, and then she smiled. 'I knew you'd come. Where's Father?'

'I'm here, darling. We've made some broth, are you hungry?'

She sniffed. 'I'd rather have trout. I haven't eaten since they captured me.' She looked around. 'What happened?'

Jack stood with her plate. 'They'd set an ambush for us, but they didn't count on your paladin's frontal assault. Frank Miller's dead.' He lowered the plate. John took it and forked a bite for her to eat. She smiled at him gratefully. 'Which one of 'em polecats hit you?' asked Jack.

She paused to recollect the encounter. 'It had to be Billy. Frank tried to get fresh and during the scuffle I got his gun. I was about to pull the hammer — that's the last I remember.'

'Well, soon as you're able to ride, I'm goin' after McCarthy. John will see you home and he'll stay there 'til I get back.'

'You sure are fond of orderin' people around,' said John.

Jack smiled. 'Only when it concerns my daughter.' He glanced at John, his grave expression held John's eyes. 'You've proved you can take care of Rebecca if there's danger, but can I trust you to be a man and take care of her as a husband should?'

Until that second, marriage was the furthest thing from John's mind. He hesitated only briefly. 'Yes, sir, you can. I don't know much about farmin', but I know how to manage a store.'

'Excuse me, but don't I have a say in this?' asked Rebecca.

John smiled at her. 'You have just one word — yes.'

With a slight blush, she glanced at Jack and then smiled at John. 'If that's a marriage proposal the answer is yes.'

The next morning, Jack saddled the dun and took most of the supplies. As he mounted, he said, 'I should be home in a couple of weeks. Tell Clark what happened, and tell him to send out Wanted posters on McCarthy. When I take 'im, I want it legal.'

14

Things didn't go the way he'd thought. It was a stupid play to kidnap McGraw's daughter, but it was done; no sense crying over spilt milk. If he could make it to Arkansas, and his people, McGraw would never get him.

The question, though, was how much head start did he have? McGraw's daughter was injured or dead. Either way, he wouldn't come after him right away. Billy figured one, maybe two days' lead; that'd be enough for him to get home where he'd be safe.

Three days of hard riding brought him into Shreveport, and he was now across the Red River and out of Texas. That fact alone, for some reason, provided him with the first comfort he'd felt in days. McCarthy rode straight for the whiskey emporiums; he needed a drink, or ten.

One of eleven children, Billy McCarthy, with urging from his parents, left home at age fifteen. His father made and sold moonshine, but revenuers discovered and destroyed his stills, so one less mouth to feed was a blessing.

Shreveport was the first large town he'd ever seen. After a few days, he found a room and board job at Madame LaBelle's Gambling Emporium for Gentlemen. The sign should have also read 'and cathouse'. Billy earned spending money as a horse holder for the patrons who stayed for only a short period of time. It was there that Billy learned the facts of life.

Once the girls found out they could make Billy blush darn near on command, there was no end of things he saw. Eighteen months or so later he'd shot up near a foot, and his voice deepened. The girls drew cards to see who would be the first to teach him the facts of life. That was over ten years ago.

He slowed as he approached what

used to be Madame LaBelle's. Now the sign read Maude's Gentlemen's Club; same trade, new owner. Inside, things hadn't changed all that much. The muted sound of a piano blended with the buzz of conversations. Heavy purple velvet curtains lined the walls and covered the windows. Billy searched the faces of the women, though he would've been surprised to recognize anyone, but still . . .

A plump, redheaded woman with her bosom bulging over the top of her green silk bodice stepped in front of him. Billy guessed her age to be between thirty-five and fifty. The cheroot she smoked flitted about as she spoke. 'What'll ya have, cowboy?'

There were three women reposed on the settee. They weren't completely naked, but not much was left to his imagination. He smiled his appreciation. 'Whiskey for now — '

Maude nodded. 'If you want a girl, you'd better pick one now. It'll get busy later, and you'll have to wait your turn.'

She looked him up and down. 'You'll have to wash first, mind ya. House rule: we don't service dirty cowboys.'

After a couple of drinks, Billy selected a dark-haired girl named Mavis to take upstairs. She collected her fee and helped him undress and wash. He got to choose a cologne from three bottles lined up on a shelf. The girl sprayed him liberally.

Billy laughed and said, 'I smell as pretty as you look, Mavis.'

Mavis giggled. Standing there with only his boots on, she thought him an attractive young man. She helped him gather his things and led him to her room.

Downstairs, a short while later, she sat with Billy, and they talked; he told her about his early days at Madame LaBelle's. His drinks began to accumulate, and before he knew it happened, he was soused. When Maude saw his condition, she showed him the door; drunks were bad for business.

With help from the lad who tended

the horses outside of Maude's, Billy found his way to a rundown boarding house in the waterfront district. It was late the next morning when he woke. Hungover, Billy, at first, couldn't remember where he'd left his horse. Slowly, the details of last night returned.

When he sat up, the room began to spin, and he felt like he was going to be sick. Several deep breaths later, the nausea passed, and he stood. The few steps to the wash basin seemed too far, but he crossed the distance. Holding his head over the basin, he poured the pitcher of water over his head and neck. Several splashes to his face and he decided he would live.

Outside, he couldn't decide if he wanted food or a drink. He decided to eat at the saloon. The nearest place to fit his needs was four blocks from the waterfront towards the centre of town. The population of Shreveport seemed to have doubled during the last ten years. Finding his way around wasn't impossible, but it proved more difficult than he'd anticipated.

Finally, he stumbled into the Red River tavern, where he ordered a beer. Billy drank it down like a man just arrived from the desert. The second, he lingered between two gulps. With the third beer, he ordered food.

'We got bacon, black beans and rice, and biscuits. The old woman might have an egg or two, but I can't say for sure.'

Billy nodded. 'Bacon, eggs, and beans and rice with biscuits is fine. I'd like some coffee, too.' The bartender acknowledged him with a gesture and disappeared for a few minutes and returned with a plate of beans and rice with a hot biscuit on the side.

'You will get the rest when it's ready,' said the bartender as he sat the plate in front of Billy. 'You look like you need food.' He winked. 'Too much fun last night?'

Billy only nodded and then tore into the plate of beans and rice. As he finished, an older woman of maybe fifty, her salt and pepper hair put up into a bun, brought the remainder of his food. He looked at the plate and then into her striking green eyes. It was obvious that she'd been a beautiful woman in her youth. He briefly wondered what life choices caused her to end up as a cook in this joint. He smiled. 'Thank you, ma'am.'

She stared down at the empty plate, which he'd polished clean with his biscuit. 'Would you like more beans and rice, sir?'

His smile changed to a grin. 'Them beans and rice was mighty good tastin', ma'am. You bet I'd like some more. And a biscuit, too, please.' She smiled back and returned to the kitchen.

Finished with breakfast, Billy poured whiskey into his coffee and leisurely thought about what he would do next. One thing was sure, he couldn't remain in Shreveport. Resolved, he gulped the last of his coffee, dropped a silver dollar on the counter and went to find his horse. Within an hour, Billy was on the trail north to Arkansas to see his kin.

Late morning the day after Billy went north, Jack rode into Shreveport. Jack spent a lot of time as he travelled, recalling everything he could about Billy McCarthy. Madame LaBelle's parlour was one of the first things he remembered. The place was a favourite topic of Billy's prison conversations.

Based on the detailed description Billy provided, Jack expected he'd be able to ride to her doorstep. He was a bit disheartened when he reined in the dun, and the sign above read Maude's. A man of about Jack's age walked out of the establishment.

'Excuse me,' called Jack, 'I'm lookin' for Madame LaBelle's place, could you tell me where it's to be found?'

The man, who dressed like a shopkeeper, looked up, startled. He stared for a moment as he digested Jack's question. He threw his thumb over his shoulder towards the front door.

'You found it, mister. Madame

LaBelle sold out to Maude a few years back.' He nodded at Jack, straightened his vest, and walked away.

It was still morning, but a whiskey to wash down the trail dust seemed appropriate enough, so he dismounted and climbed the steps to Maude's Gentlemen's Club. Compared to the evenings, the atmosphere was downright sedate. Two girls, wearing lacy lingerie, lounged on the settee, waiting for an errant morning client. They glanced at him, but their eyes didn't convey interest. Maude stepped into view, wrapping a cotton robe around her girth.

'It's kind of early, mister. We ain't got no water heated, and we don't service dirty cowboys.' She gestured with a nod at the door. 'Get a bath somewhere and then come back.'

Jack smiled at her. 'A bath is a good idea, ma'am, but for now all I want is a whiskey and some information.'

As she studied Jack, Maude took a factory-rolled cigarette from a silver plated case carried in her pocket. On the table beside the door, she took a sulfur match from a holder and stuck it against the striker on its side. The match flared as she lit the end of her smoke; she tasted the sulfur with her first inhale and grimaced. Finally, she said, 'We sell whiskey and sometimes information. What is it that you want to know?'

Still smiling, Jack walked over to a comfortable-looking chair next to a small table. 'Let me have the whiskey while I tell you what I want to know.'

Maude nodded at one of the girls, and she popped up and went to a brass and glass liquor cart placed in front of the window. She returned with a glass of whiskey and sat it on the table.

With a glance from the whiskey to Jack, she asked, 'So . . . '

Jack took a generous sip of the amber liquid. He held it in his mouth, feeling its burn and then swallowed. His intake of air felt cool as it rushed down his throat into his lungs.

'That's excellent whiskey.' His smile was genuine. He took a second smaller sip and repeated the process; the burn was much less this time. He smiled. 'I'm looking for a young man by the name of Billy McCarthy. He worked here as a kid when the place belonged to Madame LaBelle. He's tall and has a boyish grin.'

Maude nodded. 'Yeah, he was here — what's he done?'

Jack hesitated, and then he decided he'd tell her the truth. 'The sum-bitch kidnapped my daughter, and later when she tried to escape, he slammed a pistol barrel against her skull which damn near killed her. I aim to shoot 'im when I catch 'im.'

The strained brow over Maude's angry eyes gave away her opinion, but she stated it anyway. 'A man smacks his wife for too much back talk, or she throwin' a skillet is one thing, but what he done is too much. I hope you find the son of a bitch soon.' She tilted her head up looking nowhere as she thought. 'He left here sometime after midnight, drunk as a skunk. The boy out front who tends the horses will be here after lunchtime. He'll be able to give you more information on his whereabouts.'

'I'll grab a bit of food and come back later. How much do I owe you for the drink and information?'

Maude smiled, but there was no humour in it. 'They're on the house — I can't abide that kind of a man, and I wish you luck findin' him. I'll tell the boy to tell you what he knows.'

Jack stood. 'I'll get a bite to eat and I'll come back later. Thanks for your help, Maude.'

A sudden gleam of interest shone in her eyes as she raised her brow suggestively. 'I sometimes service a client personally, and I don't charge, but I'm picky. So, if you want a romp after that bath, I'd be more'n happy to oblige you.'

Caught off guard, Jack's face reddened. 'I'm flattered . . . '

15

The return to Crockett was slow. John, despite Rebecca's protests, stopped often to let her rest, and he refused to let the horses move faster than a walk. On their third morning, she said, 'John, I'm not a child. I no longer have a headache and except for tenderness to the touch, my head is fine.'

He sighed. 'All right, we'll ride all day, but we'll keep it easy for a while longer. I wouldn't want you to fall off or — '

'John!' Her eyes sparked, she'd had enough. 'Catch me if you can,' she yelled as she heeled her horse in the flanks. Used to the slow gait of previous days, her pony started and bolted to a flat-out run. She was fifty yards ahead before John and his mount could organize their pursuit.

The chase lasted for over a mile

before John's pony made up the distance. He reached out and caught her horse's bridle and slowed it to a walk and finally a standstill.

'We should get off and let them have a rest.' He glared at her. 'That was a damn fool thing to do. What if you'd fallen?'

Rebecca glared back. 'I have a father, thank you, and he has more confidence in me than you do, John Simpson.'

'How's this goin' to work if you won't do as I say?'

With her jaw set, and lips clamped tight, Rebecca stared back at John for several seconds. 'What are you talking about?' Her eyes flashed with rebelliousness.

His stare was incredulous. 'Why, our gettin' married is what.'

Rebecca laughed. It was gay, happy laughter. She hooked her arm inside his as they walked. 'John, you haven't proposed.'

'But, Rebecca, you said — '

'I know very well what I said. I said I

wouldn't marry you if you decided to earn your way with a gun.'

John hung his head. 'Don't it mean we're gettin' married since I told you I'd work for my pa and learn to be a farmer?'

She looked away to conceal the smile that crossed her face. 'No, it doesn't, you have to propose properly.'

'You're goin' to say yes, ain't you?'

'You'll have to propose and find out.'

'Good grief,' he said, and then sighed loudly. He turned to halt the horses and still holding their reins he dropped to one knee. 'Miss Rebecca Gott — um, McGraw, will you marry me?'

She grinned at him as he waited on his knee.

'Why?' she asked. The shocked look on his face caused her to break out into hysterical laughter. John could only look on bewildered. Finally, she caught her breath. 'Of course, I'll marry you. I want that more than anything in the world.'

'So you were havin' fun at my

expense, that it? Why, if you weren't hurt, I'd bend you over my knee and whale the daylights out of your backside.' He jumped up and took a step towards her.

Startled, she jumped back. 'You wouldn't dare.'

'Just you be sure to never give me cause,' he said and then he remounted his horse and waited for her to mount.

She glanced up at him with an impish grin. 'I guess I'm well enough to mount without your help.' He leaned over, grabbing her under her arms and lifted her into the air and slung her on to her horse. The whole motion happened so quickly Rebecca had no chance to complain. Once she settled and straightened her clothes, she said, 'Thank you, dear.'

★   ★   ★

Late that evening, John and Rebecca arrived at Crockett. John's father's store was closed, so they rode around to the

174

house in the rear. His parents came out to the porch to greet them.

'John, Rebecca, you're both safe,' said Sarah. She held her hands clasped near her mouth and fought back tears.

Robert hurried down the steps and helped Rebecca dismount. He looked past them and asked, 'Where's McGraw?'

John dismounted and as he helped Rebecca, he said, 'He was fine the last we saw of him. Miller's dead and Jack's after McCarthy. Rebecca was hurt, so I brought her back to Crockett.'

Sarah rushed down the steps, taking Rebecca's hands and turning her around for inspection. 'Where are you hurt, dear? Is it serious?' She leaned in close and whispered, 'They didn't . . . '

'No, Mother, they didn't,' said John. 'Billy McCarthy clubbed her with his pistol when she tried to escape.'

'Oh my word, dear,' said Sarah. 'Come into the house and we'll get you cleaned up. Robert, go fetch Doctor Benson.'

'Please, there's no need to go for the

doctor, I'm fine, but I would like to clean up if I may.'

'But a blow to the head is dangerous,' continued Sarah. 'Go on and fetch the doctor, Robert.' He shrugged and walked away.

Sarah guided Rebecca into the house, leaving John to deal with the horses. Inside, she helped Rebecca to disrobe and brought her fresh water for the washstand basin. 'I've some clothes from when I was younger that I'm sure will fit. You wait here and let me see what I can find.'

Rebecca was alone for the first time in several days. As she waited, she reflected. *Whew, what a time; I've learned that I have a father, I've been kidnapped, nearly killed, and now I'm engaged.* Aloud she said, 'I couldn't be happier.'

'Happier about what, dear?' asked Sarah as she returned with a complete set of clothes for Rebecca. 'These should do nicely.'

Rebecca quickly dressed. The dress was a little loose, but then she'd not eaten much for several days. 'Thank you so much.'

'Hello,' called Robert from the kitchen. 'Doc Benson's here.'

Sarah brought Rebecca out and sat her down at the kitchen table. 'I'll make some tea while the doctor examines your head.'

By the time the tea was ready, Doc Benson completed his examination. 'You're fine, young lady, but I want you to take it easy for a few more days. Leastways 'til that bump's gone. If you have any dizziness or feel faint, you send someone to fetch me.'

John came in. Everyone stopped to stare and for whatever reason, he blushed.

'Did you tell 'em already?'

'Tell us what?' asked Sarah, looking from John to Rebecca.

Rebecca shook her head. 'I was waiting for you.'

Everyone again stared at John. 'Aw, hell. Rebecca and me is goin' to get married as soon as things can be arranged.'

The room fell silent. Sarah and Robert,

mouths agape, stared at each other. Finally, Doc Benson stepped across the room and extended his hand. 'That's wonderful news, John. I couldn't be more pleased for the both of you.'

Doc's actions broke the spell that seemed to have frozen John's parents. Sarah leaned down to hug Rebecca. 'This is wonderful news, dear. Welcome to the family.'

Robert rushed across the room and slapped his son on the shoulder, and then grabbed his hand and began to vigorously pump his arm, unable to control his excitement.

'About time you asked her. Why, darn near the whole town's been wonderin' when you'd get up the nerve.'

John and Rebecca exchanged glances. He said, 'It wasn't lack of courage holdin' me back, it was stupidity. The thought of losing Rebecca scared me so bad it changed my thinkin'.'

The room went quiet and became awkward after John's declaration of his feelings for Rebecca.

Sarah sighed, and said, 'My word. You children must be hungry and Rebecca, you need to get some rest. After you've eaten, you can sleep in John's room.' She looked at John with hooded eyes. 'I'll make a pallet on the floor in here for him to sleep.'

John grinned, moved to his mother's side and put his arm around her shoulders and squeezed. 'After so many nights on the trail,' he said, 'it'll feel like a down mattress.'

Sarah busied herself in the kitchen, slicing bread and ham for sandwiches. As John and Rebecca ate those, she brought out an apple pie and served them each a generous portion.

Rebecca, joined by Sarah, sat at the table sipping their tea. Robert stepped away to the cupboard and returned with a bottle of bonded whiskey.

'I think it's time we shared a drink, son.' He splashed the liquor into their glasses. 'What're your plans?'

John sipped his whiskey. 'I promised Jack that I'd get Rebecca back home and stay with her until he returns.'

'Nonsense,' said Sarah. 'She'll stay right here until her father gets back. I'll hear nothing further on the matter.'

'I'm sorry, Mrs Simpson, a farm is more than just a house. It and the animals need tending. We've been gone for several days as it is — ' Her expression shone with worry.

'Don't fret, Rebecca,' said John. 'I'll do as I promised. We'll head out early in the mornin'. You'll have to explain things for a while, but we'll do fine.'

'But — ' Sarah began. Robert's stern look stayed her comment. She sighed. 'If you must, dear, but you two can't be out there all alone; I'll go out there with you.'

★   ★   ★

Jack left Maude's place intent on getting that bath, food, and another drink; pretty much in that order. A local barber shop provided a bath for two bits.

'Shave and a haircut is another two bits,' said the painfully thin young man.

'You been at this barber business long?' asked Jack as he studied the barber. His thinness made him appear taller than his real height. The smile was genuine enough, but his eyes bulged and made him look like a marionette. His dark unruly hair appeared like he cut it himself.

'A few years now,' said the barber. 'Went to barber college in Indiana and graduated fifth in the class.'

Jack smiled. 'How many in the class?'

The barber stared for a moment and then understanding came into his eyes. 'Very funny, sir, but I'll have you know that there were eighty-six students in my class.'

The smile grew to a grin. 'OK, I was just askin',' said Jack.

Later, freshly bathed and shaved, Jack McGraw stood on the town's boardwalk and surveyed his food and drink opportunities. He spied a sign that read: Belle's Cajun Emporium. Smoke rose from a chimney at the rear which suggested a kitchen. As he drew nearer, a wonderful aroma confirmed his suspicion.

Jack peeked over the batwing doors. The saloon had two more employees than patrons. The savoury smell that attracted Jack's attention in the first place wafted from their kitchen, through the saloon, and out the door. He followed his nose inside and sat at a table near the kitchen.

Once inside, Jack gave more attention to the interior of Belle's establishment. Rich red mahogany panelled the walls and where they joined the ceiling, the cornices were trimmed with ornate plaster moldings. Heavy red curtains sectioned off the wall, giving the impression of compartments.

The building was wider than the typical saloons of Jack's experience. The main bar ran nearly the length of the room. Tables and chairs placed closely together filled the centre. Against the opposite wall were the gambling tables;

faro and roulette. Towards the rear of the saloon, they'd built a small performance stage with a lower platform to the side for a band.

At the bar, a younger man leaned on his elbows, staring out of the window. One of the dance girls, the more experienced of the two based on the many lines on her face, sat at a table with the only other patron. Jack had noticed another girl . . . 'Hello,' said a sweet and warm sounding voice. 'You look lonely. Would you like some company?'

Jack started to say no, thanks, but when he looked up at her face, he just stared, saying nothing. It was her deep blue eyes; not the colour, but the way she looked at him, she seemed to penetrate his being. Not since his Rebecca had any woman had that effect on him. He smiled, and said, 'Please do.' And rose from his seat and held out his hand to guide her into the chair.

Colour pinked her cheeks as she cast her eyes down. 'Thank you,' she said.

'It's been a very long while since a gentleman held my chair for me.'

Jack's smile broadened to a toothy grin, and then he said, 'I find that hard to believe, Miss, er . . . '

'Nancy, Nancy Lowe and you are . . . '

He moved to his side of the table and sat. 'It's John William McGraw, but my friends call me Jack.' He appraised her features. Her long neck, smooth shoulders, tiny waist, and creamy-white skin; there was not one single thing that was unique or overly outstanding, but in total, she was beautiful.

'May I call you Jack, Mr McGraw?'

'I'd be mighty disappointed if you didn't, Nancy.'

Nancy glanced at the young man tending the bar; he stared at her with an expectant expression and gave a slight nod.

She understood what the gesture meant. Her cheeks flushed as she briefly glanced away. She turned back and asked, 'Would you like to buy me a drink, Jack?'

Jack glanced at the bartender and then back to her. 'I'd rather buy you breakfast and coffee, but if it's to be a drink, then by all means, I'd be delighted.'

She rose and went to the bar, where their drinks waited. When she returned to the table, she pointedly made sure which drink was hers. 'If you'd like breakfast I can order you a plate.'

His smile said yes. 'And coffee.'

Nancy ducked through the kitchen door and brought back a plate filled with red beans and rice, sausages, and two biscuits. As she placed the plate in front of him, she said, 'They're brewing a fresh pot of coffee. It'll be out in a minute.'

The food's aroma rose from the plate, which caused Jack's stomach to churn with pangs of hunger. He glanced at the food, hesitated, and then looked to Nancy. She said, 'Please don't mind me. You go ahead and eat — it's good food.'

She was right, the food was good and

it had a spicy kick. He looked for the bartender. Seeing him, Jack called, 'Beer.'

Nancy met the bartender halfway and returned with Jack's beer. 'I should've warned you it tends to be spicy.'

Jack drank nearly half the beer. 'I like spicy, but I wasn't prepared for this much heat. Still, it's awfully good.'

After Jack finished his meal and consumed another beer, he settled back to sip his whiskey and enjoy Nancy's company. 'I hope you don't take this wrong, but you seem to be new at working in a dancehall.'

'It's that obvious? Well, yes, this is my first week.'

He waited for her to continue, but she said nothing more.

'How'd you come to work here?' asked Jack.

She didn't speak immediately; rather she stared deeply into his eyes, trying to discern his motive. Jack's eyes conveyed nothing beyond an honest interest in her. She said, 'I answered an advertisement and came out here from Ohio. Things didn't work out and I don't have the funds to return home, so I took a job here.' She laughed, but it held little humour. 'I'm not very experienced, so Charlie assigned me to work during the day.'

Jack studied her intently. He'd heard his share of hard luck stories, and he wondered if it was a ploy, so he asked, 'What's back in Ohio that you want to go back to — family?'

'No family,' she said. 'But I've friends and maybe my old job. I worked in a hospital as a nurse.' Jack smiled and watched her as she spoke. She blushed. 'I came out here in reply to an offer of marriage.' Her cheeks burned again, and she cast her eyes downward. 'That's so silly; a woman of my age.'

He reached across the table and laid a hand on hers. 'I don't think that's silly at all.' He smiled when she looked up.

Jack's comment released her inhibitions, and her story followed. 'He was a widowed doctor. It seemed natural to me that he'd want a wife who was also a nurse.' He nodded for her to continue. 'Walter — Doctor Morgan turned out to be considerably older than I was led to believe. Worse, though, was his attitude about women in medicine.' Her jaw flexed and her eyes squinted. 'It was fine for me to bathe patients and change their bedpans, but that was all he allowed. I was trained by Clara Barton during the end of the War and worked in a hospital as a surgeon's assistant until I left to come out here. Why I — '

'I see,' interrupted Jack. His eyes twinkled with suppressed laughter. 'So you want to go back to the hospital in Ohio?'

She stopped her rant and stared at Jack. She smiled. 'I apologize. I get worked up about the situation.'

'Do you want to go back?' asked Jack again.

Nancy gave a large sigh. 'Not really, but I don't know what else I'm to do. I mean, I'm not very good at this sort of work. The men who come in here seem to resent my efforts to be nice.'

'I don't — maybe you're trying too hard?'

'Or not hard enough! The men are drunk and smelly at night. During the day, they only want something to eat and a beer. Belle pays me pennies for each drink I entice a patron to buy, and I earn tips if they want to dance. At the rate I'm going, I'll be an old woman before I save enough money to return to Ohio.' Despite her beleaguered situation, she laughed.

The words came out before he even knew the idea was present in his mind. 'Nancy, have dinner with me tonight,' he blurted; the shocked expression on his face nearly compared to her's.

After she regained her composure, she said, 'Jack, I'm flattered, really I am, but I don't know you. I don't — '

'It's only a meal in a public place,' he pressed. 'What time are you through here, or should I meet you elsewhere?'

She stared into Jack's eager eyes. There was nothing to support her fearful feelings, but she liked and for some reason trusted Jack McGraw. Things had been rough these past few weeks, and she was entitled to something positive happening in her life. A smile creased her face, and her eyes flashed with girlish excitement. 'I have a room upstairs. There's a rear entrance, you can wait at the bottom of the stairs. I'll be ready by 6.30.'

Early in the afternoon, Jack returned to Maude's. A boy stood outside the house, tending to their clients' horses. As Jack approached him, the boy said, 'You must be the man who wants the information about the cowboy too drunk to ride.'

Jack's brow wrinkled as he stared at the boy. 'How'd — '

'You ain't got no horse, mister. Men come here to see the women, not visit me, so it had to figure.'

The smile on Jack's face showed his admiration. 'You're a smart lad — you'll

go far.' The boy shrugged. Jack continued, 'What can you tell me about the
drunk?'

'Ain't much to tell. The gent could
hardly walk, so I took 'im to a boardin'
house near the river. He showed up
here the next day hungover. I could
smell whiskey, but he could ride.'

'Which way did he head?'

'North. His head must've still been
hurtin', 'cause it was at a slow walk, a
mighty slow walk.'

Jack smiled as he gathered his
thoughts, *a day ahead*.

16

At 6.15, Jack waited at the foot of the stairs leading up to Nancy's room. When the door opened and she came through at exactly 6.30, he at first didn't recognize her. She dressed so differently; her blouse was buttoned at her throat, and the skirt and jacket were a deep blue colour that complemented her eyes. Beneath her hat, she wore her hair pinned up; curly locks cascaded over her left shoulder. Then he saw her eyes.

Jack, who'd purchased a new shirt, suddenly felt under-dressed. On impulse, he wiped the toes of his boots on the back of his trousers. 'Nancy, you look beautiful; I didn't recognize you.'

She halted a few steps from the bottom. Her stare was pensive. 'Oh! Is that right?'

His mouth dropped open, he'd said

that badly and now knew it. 'That's not what I meant, Nancy. I mean, of course you're beautiful all the time, but you look so different — elegant.' He stared up at her with pleading eyes.

She broke out into laughter. 'That was an excellent recovery; I forgive you. Now, where are we going for dinner?'

'I thought since you're from Ohio, you might like a change from the local diet. Do you like Chinese food?'

'I don't know. Shall we try it and see?'

She came down the last few steps and took his arm. Jack led her up the alley on to the main street, and then left, away from the saloon.

The atmosphere at Ming's Chinese restaurant was unlike anything they'd ever seen. Owned and managed by three generations of a Chinese family, who all dressed in traditional clothing, they spoke English to the clientele and Chinese among themselves. Their rapid-fire speech had a sing-song element to it, and everyone rushed about, creating a sense of urgency. The patrons ate quickly, paid their bill, and left the restaurant, so the family could serve new customers.

All that is, except Jack and Nancy. After several questions concerning the food, they ordered. As the waitress left their table, Nancy said, 'If the food isn't any good, at least the floor show is entertaining.'

Jack turned to watch the family rush about speaking Chinese while they worked.

Nancy said, 'I'd be exhausted if I worked here. How do they maintain the pace?'

With dinner finished, they ignored the commotion going on around them and quietly talked, all the while sipping their tea. Eventually, the white-haired grandmother came to their table.

'You go home now — we close!' She thrust the bill into his face.

Jack looked up at the wall clock hung behind the counter. 'It's nine o'clock. I didn't realize the time.' He glanced at the bill and left twice the amount shown. Outside, he asked, 'Would you care to take a stroll before I take you home?'

They walked under the street lamps and found themselves at the courthouse, where they sat on one of the many benches provided for the citizenry of Shreveport. There they talked until nearly dawn.

'I can't believe I've told you so much about me,' said Jack. He looked eastward at the grey sky and sighed.

'Nor I about me,' agreed Nancy. 'It must have been all the tea we drank. It's stronger than any coffee I've had.'

'I have this business with McCarthy to deal with.' He paused and stared deeply into Nancy's eyes. She didn't look away. 'I know this sounds stupid, but I've wasted too much of my life, and well, would you marry me?'

She too felt the chemistry between them, but marriage after just an evening's conversation? Yet, hadn't she travelled all this way to marry a man based on a few letters?

'Jack, I — '

'Don't answer me now. Let me send you to Crockett with a letter to my daughter. Wait for me there and when my business is finished, we'll work things out. If we can't, then I'll send you back home to Ohio. What do you say?'

'It seems so preposterous, Jack. There are so many things — '

'Just say yes, and I'll put you on a stage today.'

Nancy stared at Jack as she pondered the myriad of things he'd told her about himself. She couldn't claim that he hid anything, but why was she holding back? Was it the fear of disappointment? What did she have to lose? A broken heart, she thought. Finally, she sighed, and said, 'Jack, I'll go, but I won't stay at your farm. I'll find work and get a room at the hotel, or if there is one at a boarding house.'

Jack's smile was filled with relief. 'I have a better idea. I'll give you a letter to Robert Simpson. He'll give you room and board in exchange for working in his store. It'll just be for a short period, and then when I return we can marry.'

The day was a tornado of activity, but by late afternoon, Jack put Nancy on a stage bound for Crockett, Texas.

* * *

Billy McCarthy rode through Bradley, Arkansas. He recognized no one he saw and none seemed to know him. There was seldom eye contact and the few he made were suspicious glares. Jack McGraw would not find anyone here to help him.

The town hadn't changed since he was last home, which hardly surprised him. There'd never been much in the way of ambition among the folks in Bradley. Though the train stopped at Bradley, no one ever got off to stay. Westward folks cleared the trees and planted crops. To the east were the same tall pines as when he left town.

His thoughts drifted to his parents' cabin by Lake Erling; were they even still alive?

Two hours later, Billy sat his horse at the edge of the clearing where his parents' cabin stood; beyond was the lake. A trail of smoke rose from the chimney; someone was home. As he approached, he called, 'Hello, the cabin!' There was no response. He looked around, maybe they were out in the woods or down by the lake.

'Anyone here?' he asked.

A gun port built into the heavy timber door swung open, and a rifle barrel poked through. 'State your business, mister.' The man's voice was deep and held a baleful edge.

'I'm looking for the McCarthy family.'

'What fer?' The rifle barrel slid further out.

Billy heard a faint metallic click. 'I'm Billy McCarthy.'

The rifle barrel pulled back, but the gun port remained opened. Finally, he heard the crossbar scrape as it cleared the door. Hammered strap hinges groaned as the door swung open. A man, still holding a rifle, stepped out.

Billy's brow creased as he studied the man's hairy face. It was lean with hard blue eyes. The man strongly resembled Billy's father.

'Is that you, Earl?' asked Billy.

The man lowered his rifle. 'It's me — what're ya doin' here?'

A smile creased Billy's face and he stood in the saddle, preparing to dismount. 'I come home for a visit.'

'Stay where ya are, you ain't welcome here.'

Billy's smile faded and was replaced by a hard stare. 'Where's Pa? We'll see what he has to say about that.'

'Dead — Ma, too; it's been four or five years now.'

The news shocked Billy. He hadn't been particularly close to his parents, but hearing that they were dead . . . suddenly, his own mortality loomed large before him and his mind flashed on Jack McGraw and what would happen if they met.

Billy and Earl, Earl being the oldest, never got along. Pa favoured him while their ma doted on Billy. Each was jealous of the other. 'So, half the farm's mine?'

'You'd be wrong about that, brother. Pa left me everythin'.'

Billy stiffened. 'Ma wouldn't let Pa do that.'

'Ma weren't around to stop 'im. She died first.'

'You got a piece of paper to that effect?' asked Billy.

'Don't need one — there was witnesses when Pa died. I own it, such as it is. Ain't nothin' ya can do about it neither.'

His shoulders slumped and his expression followed. 'Earl, I'd like to stay a few days and rest up.'

Earl sneered, and said, 'Not likely, Billy. Word got back to Ma about you bein' in jail. The news broke her heart; her health became poorly, and she died.

You ain't welcomed here — now git!'
Earl aimed the rifle's barrel at Billy and
cocked the hammer. 'I won't tell ya no
more, so git — ya hear?'

'Earl, I can file papers with Lawyer
Diggs for my share. I know he's still
around 'cause I saw his shingle hangin'
in front of the buildin' next to the
general store.'

Billy saw murder in Earl's eyes. 'I
warned ya — '

'Wait! There's another way. If you'll
let me stay a few days, I'll sign papers
givin' you my half of the place free and
clear.'

Earl hesitated, and then slowly
lowered his rifle. 'Ya can stay a week
— no longer.' He nodded towards the
cabin. 'There's pen and paper inside.
Get to writin'.'

* * *

Jack didn't recall the name of Billy's
hometown at first, but when he saw
the signpost pointing to Bradley, he

remembered the stories Billy told about getting to go into town with his mother to buy their monthly supplies. Being the youngest, he was his mother's pet. As Billy told it, his father and brother were jealous of him and his relationship with his mother.

Bradley was a rural farm town. Its businesses were what Jack expected; a feed store, blacksmith, dry goods, barber shop, town marshal's office, a doctor, and two saloons. Jack rode to the more prosperous looking of the two and tied up outside.

It was just after noon, and customers were few. Jack walked the length of the bar and took a position where he could watch the room and the entrance. Nicer than its competitor, the saloon was crudely built from pine timbers, including its bar. Kerosene lamps hung from cords above. They lowered them each night at dusk to be lit and were extinguished during the day. There was nothing behind the bar except shelves for liquor and glasses, both collecting dust.

The bartender asked, 'What'll it be?'

'Beer — can a man get somethin' to eat here?'

The bartender set his beer in front of him. 'If you ain't too picky, I kin see what they got in the kitchen.'

Jack didn't smile, but he kept his expression pleasant.

'That'll do fine.' He downed his beer and gestured for another.

The bartender brought him sliced pork between slices of bread. The bread wasn't stale, but it certainly wasn't fresh, but he was too hungry to really care. He washed each bite down with a swallow of beer.

'One more beer,' Jack said.

As the bartender sat a fresh beer in front of him, Jack said, 'I'm lookin' for a friend of mine, name of Billy McCarthy. His folks got a farm out east of town — that right?'

The bartender stared at him, his expression blank. 'I mind my own business, and so does most everyone else around 'ere.'

Finally, slight curls came to the corners of Jack's mouth. He nodded, and said, 'That's what Billy said. I wouldn't have to worry about anyone finding me here.' Jack laid a twenty dollar gold piece on the bar. 'Can you tell me the way out to Erling Lake? I mean the first road out of town that goes to the lake.'

The bartender looked around the bar; no one seemed to be paying any attention to him, so he slid the coin off the bar top and slipped it into his pocket. He leaned towards Jack . . .

⋆   ⋆   ⋆

Billy penned the transfer of his half of the farm to Earl. 'We need a witness for my signature.'

Earl called, 'Martha, you and the boys can come out now.'

The door to the bedroom his parents shared for as long as he could remember swung open, and a raw-boned woman with stringy blonde hair stepped out.

Behind her, clinging to her skirt, were two young boys Billy guessed to be six and eight years old. She stared at him, and an expectation shone in her eyes.

Then it came to him; this was Martha Seaward. She was a year or so younger than he, and they'd played together as children. He glanced at Earl.

'You and Martha got married?'

Earl didn't answer; an angry stare was his reply.

Martha finger combed her hair and said, 'Hello, Billy.'

She looks so different from the handsome teenage girl of ten years past, he thought. He did the maths; she was twenty-five or six, but she looked forty. Billy forced a smile.

'Martha, ah — it's good to see you again, too.'

'Don't just stand there gaping, get over here and sign this paper,' said Earl, his tone gruff and his manner threatening. Martha flinched and scurried over to the table. She paused to read its content and then glanced at Billy. Earl slapped her bottom and added, 'You don't need to know what it says, just sign it.'

'Take it easy, Earl,' said Billy, 'there ain't no call — '

'She's my wife — mind your own business.' Martha slinked away to her boys, who watched the interaction with guarded anticipation, ready to dart back into the room. Earl gestured at them and all three left the room.

'Kind of rough on your family, Earl. It ain't on my account?'

Earl sneered at Billy. 'Martha's not too smart and both the boys are idiots. They just stare, never sayin' a word.'

'She seemed smart enough when we was in school, and — '

'Like I said, Billy, you tend to your business, and I'll look after me and mine.' Earl's hard look ended the discussion.

17

Jack stood on the boardwalk outside the saloon. Absently, he'd pulled the knight from his pocket and traced its features with his finger as he considered his next move.

'Do you play?' Jack looked around and a tall, lanky man who looked to be Jack's age was staring at the chess piece.

'I do,' said Jack, 'but it's been a while.'

'Care to play a game, Mr uh?' The man smiled and extended his hand. 'My name's Zach Johnson, I'm the town's legal man.'

Jack took the offered hand. 'Jack McGraw and yes, I'd like to play a game. You said the town's legal man?'

An easy grin spread across Johnson's face. 'I'm the town lawyer, justice of the peace, and county clerk. My office is across the street, and my chess board is ready to go.'

Jack followed as Zach led the way to his office. It was a ground floor office sectioned off from a two storey building. The other half stood empty. Inside there were stairs in the rear, which Jack supposed lead to living quarters above. Beyond the main counter at the entrance were book shelves and file cabinets. In the centre of the space sat a large walnut banker's desk, and behind it were the game table and two chairs.

The pieces were carved bone; the patina told Jack they were old. He picked up the four-inch-high king. 'This is a nice set.'

Zach smiled, obviously pleased that Jack admired the set. 'My grandfather was a whaler. He carved the entire set. When he died, my father inherited them. We moved here when I was a child. Then, when my father passed, they came to me.'

With a brown and white pawn in

either hand, Zach put his hands behind his back and switched the pieces several times. Finally, he offered Jack a choice.

Jack touched Zach's left hand. He opened it and revealed the brown pawn. Zach had the whites and the first move. Their first game was quick with Zach achieving checkmate in six moves. The second game went much slower, resulting in a stalemate. As they set up the pieces for their third game, Zach said, 'There's somethin' about you — I knew you'd give me a good game.'

'We'll see,' said Jack as he moved a pawn to counter Zach's initial move. Zach paused only the slightest moment, but Jack saw the hesitation. He smiled at Zach. 'We'll see indeed.'

Twenty-five minutes later, Jack said, 'Checkmate!'

With gracious laughter, Zach laid his king on its side. 'You've beaten me fair and square. I've studied a lot about chess and I've never seen anything about your opening move.'

It was Jack's turn to feel pleased, and

his grin showed it. 'The man who taught me to play also read a great deal about chess. Kurt developed the strategy for that opening.'

'Kurt who? I'd like to meet this man.'

Jack's eyes saddened as he looked at Zach. 'His name is Kurt Jager, but I'm afraid meeting him ain't possible.'

Seeing Jack's saddened expression, Zach made the wrong assumption about Kurt's existence. 'I'm sorry for your loss. He must have been a grand fellow and a good friend.'

Jack's brow pinched as he stared at Zach. 'He's not dead — he's in prison serving a life sentence for murder.'

Zach's eyes and mouth opened wide, and he stared. Finally, he snapped his jaw closed. 'I just assumed anyone who played chess that well would be a gentleman at least and — '

The laughter from Jack made Zach blush. 'Zach, I assumed anyone who lived in Bradley would be more savvy about the lower classes.'

'In my defence,' Zach smiled, too, 'I

don't know anyone of the lower classes that can play chess. It's a gentleman's game.'

'Correction, Zach, it's a thinkin' man's game.'

After several seconds, Zach asked, 'How did you come to know Mr Jager. Did you work at the prison where he resides?'

'Nope, wrong again.' Jack liked Zach and for whatever reason felt he was not judgmental and could be trusted. 'I shared a cell with him for eighteen years.'

Zach's expression was more of curiosity than wonder. 'Really! Again, I assumed that — ' He clamped his mouth closed.

'It's all right, Zach. I'm a different person now. Not because of prison, at least not directly because of prison; Kurt made me a better man. He used this game to teach me more about life and people than I could have ever learned by myself.'

'May I inquire as to the circumstances that caused your incarceration?'

Zach leaned closer to hear Jack's words.

After hearing the entire story, Zach said, 'That was not justice. You should have pursued a new trial. I'm confident that you would not have been convicted the second time.'

'It's kind of you to say, Zach, but that ship's long sailed.'

Zach stood and stepped over to the book shelves and returned with a bottle of rye and two glasses.

'I know it's a bit early, but would you care to join me?' Jack nodded and Zach poured generously. 'I don't mean to seem overly nosy, but what brings you to Bradley? We don't get many strangers here.'

'I'm lookin' for a man, name of Billy McCarthy,' Jack shared the whole story with Zach.

Jack could see from Zach's expression that he was considering whether to get involved or not. At length, he said, 'There's an Earl McCarthy that lives near Erling Lake.'

'That'd be Billy's brother. What

about their parents?'

'They died a while back. Left everything to Earl, according to witnesses at the father's death. I drew up the documents.'

'Hmm,' said Jack, 'I bet Billy took that news as a comfort.' Jack rubbed the stubble on his chin. 'As I recall, he and his brother didn't get along all that well; seems Billy made the most of bein' his mother's favourite. Earl and his pa objected.'

'I could tell there was no love lost with Earl. After I recorded the documents, Earl was too overjoyed given the circumstances. He offered to buy me a drink to celebrate.'

'Have you been out to their place?' asked Jack.

Deep lines creased Zach's forehead, and then it smoothed as his eyes shone with cognition. 'Yes, I have. It's been a few years, but I was out there to serve a tax notice — why?'

Jack studied Zach's face searching his eyes. Finally, he said, 'I mean to see him in jail or dead for what he did to my daughter.' He shook his head and slowed his breathing to curtail the rising anger growing in his chest. 'Zach, I need directions on how to get to their farm and any information you can remember about its layout. Can you provide that?'

The pensive expression on Zach's face made Jack's anticipation of a positive response weaken. After nearly a full minute, Zach sighed. 'Folks hereabouts don't give information to outsiders. Aw hell, I've lived here over twenty years and they still hush up when I walk by.'

Jack smiled and gave a knowing nod. 'Then you'll help me?'

'I don't see why not.' Zach paused to take a deep breath, and started, 'You take the north road . . . '

* * *

Very early the next morning, Jack mounted up and rode north out of town with the intent of scouting the McCarthy farm before making his move to take Billy. The moist cool breeze told him he neared the lake; he slowed his horse. Around a bend, he saw the edge of a clearing. He rode into the trees and dismounted. After he hitched his horse, Jack made his way towards McCarthy's farm.

The house was awake; its occupants moved about the yard performing chores. The melancholy was palpable; no one moved quickly or spoke. They most certainly didn't smile; even the animals seemed listless. Jack wondered why anyone would want to live in such a place if it made them that unhappy.

A tall, muscular man with a dark beard came out of the cabin and made his way to the privy. Behind him in the doorway stood Billy, who watched the woman and her children; he was unarmed.

Jack stepped out from the trees, gun drawn. 'Move, Billy, and I'll kill you where you stand.'

Billy's eyes grew wide, showing the whites. He glanced at the privy. In a voice louder than necessary, he said, 'McGraw.'

With a motion of his gun, Jack signalled for Billy to come out into the yard. Again, he stole a glance at the privy, and then walked out of the cabin. Three paces from the doorway, Jack said, 'That's far enough.' He raised his voice so he could be heard and said, 'You in the outhouse, stay put until we've gone. If I see that door move, I'll start blastin'. You got that?'

The voice was muffled, but plain. 'I heard ya.'

Jack looked at the oldest boy. 'Where's his horse?'

He pointed at a tired old shack, and said, 'In the barn.'

'You and your brother bring him out — '

He'd forgotten about the woman. From the corner of his eye, a movement made him duck just as a chuck of firewood glanced off his shoulder; pain

216

numbed his arm and shoulder. Jack whirled ready to fire, but checked his action when he saw it was the woman. She turned and ran to the barn.

Meanwhile, Billy saw his chance and rushed Jack. As he threw himself at Jack he called, 'Earl, now — help me!'

Jack went down backwards, but retained his grip on his pistol, which he shoved into Billy's gut and pulled the trigger. Billy moaned and rolled off Jack, who then swung his gun arm around to face Earl. The big man froze in his tracks and raised his hands.

'Easy, mister, I don't want to get shot.'

Gut shot, Billy curled into a foetal position. He repeated several times, 'You've kilt me, damn you, you've kilt me.'

Getting to his feet, Jack turned to Earl. 'It'd be best if you went to the barn with your wife and children.'

Earl nodded and walked past Billy without looking at him as he went to the barn. Jack knelt by Billy and inspected the wound; it bled profusely. The bullet severed an artery.

'Billy, I meant to take you back. You shouldn't have jumped me like that.' Billy stopped moaning. Jack called to the barn, 'You can come out now.'

Earl stepped out alone. 'What do you plan to do now, mister?'

'Billy was wanted for kidnapping, he gave me no choice.'

'You must be McGraw, the one who's been chasing him — that right?'

Jack nodded. 'But I meant to take him back to stand trial.'

'It don't make no difference to me,' said Earl. 'He never was any good. I'll bury him next to Ma — that's what she'd of wanted.'

Earl went into the barn and came out with a shovel. He moved towards Jack and Billy's dead form. Jack stepped back, giving Earl plenty of room. The big man wrestled Billy's body on to his shoulder and walked off towards a fenced-off willow tree. Jack melted back into the trees to his horse.

18

Simpson worked the broom with great zeal as if once and for all he'd remove the debris that collected on the boardwalk in front of his store. Nancy Lowe watched him work through the storefront's window; she laughed and shook her head.

'That section of boardwalk is thinner than any in town.'

A farmer's wife, who sorted through the store's bolts of cloth, looked up and followed Nancy's gaze. 'You'd think he was earnin' wages. That man wears out a broom every six months.'

'He sweeps it every morning; even when it rains. I've asked him why, but he don't have a good answer other than 'it needs it'.'

The woman customer adjusted her shawl. 'I'd like four yards of the floral print.'

Nancy left Robert to his sweeping and tended to the woman. Outside, Robert passed the window, lost to view to those inside. He'd just finished his morning task and looked towards the north end of town. He did a double-take, leaned his broom against the building, bolted off the porch, and ran up the street.

'Jack, you're back — did you get him?'

A tired smile grew on Jack's face. 'Howdy, Robert, it's good to be back. Did Miss Lowe arrive all right? Is she at the store?'

'She's there, Jack. I'm sure goin' to be sorry when you two get hitched. Business has doubled since she came to the store.'

'And Rebecca?' asked Jack, his direct stare expectant.

'She's fine, Jack. The missus and John are stayin' with her out at the farm. They was just in the other day for supplies.'

Jack closed his eyes and exhaled

deeply. He slumped in the saddle, letting Robert lead his horse by the bridle. 'I could sleep for a week,' he paused, 'right after I eat my horse.'

'I'll take you around to my house and tell Nancy you're here, then you can do both; she's a fair cook, too.'

Sipping warmed coffee, Jack nearly spilled it, startled by the front door bursting open. Nancy rushed forward and had her arms around his neck before he could rise.

'You're back. I was so worried, why didn't you send word? Rebecca is lovely, and the town's welcomed me with open arms. John's such a wonder the way he takes care of her and the way he works the farm, and — '

'Whoa — ' said Jack as he tried to detangle himself from her embrace. 'I'm back now, and for good, so sit and tell me what I've missed, but talk slower, please.'

Nancy neither sat nor spoke slower; she prepared Jack something to eat and talked all the while. By the time he finished the meal, she had brought him current with events.

Jack sat back from the table with his cup of coffee; he was less tired now. 'Have you had any trouble from Page?'

'Mr Page? Why would he cause trouble? I only know of him from the store, but he seems a respectable sort.'

His hesitation caused her to stop and stare. He said, 'It was his men who kidnapped Rebecca. I don't know why, but he wants the farm; maybe bad enough to kill to get it.'

'I had no idea. No one said anything like that to me.'

For the first time Jack realized that only he and Rebecca suspected Ben Page of being behind their trouble.

'I guess that's because it's not known by many.' He paused to consider. 'The sheriff knows there's a problem, but that's about all.'

'And you don't have any idea why Mr Page wants the farm?'

'Not a clue, Nancy. It's a nice little farm, though a portion of it sits on bedrock where nothin' but scrub will grow.' Like most farmers, he had a practical outlook about land. 'I guess if you have a little good, you need a little bad to appreciate it.'

He yawned involuntarily and stretched his tired muscles. Nancy rose and stood beside him with an arm across his shoulders.

'Why don't you lie down for a spell? I'll wake you in a couple of hours.' She helped him stand and led him to John's room, where he flopped across the bed, asleep without removing his boots.

When he opened his eyes, the light cast through the bedroom window was orange and fading. He'd slept several hours. As he stretched, he wiggled his toes. He looked down at his feet and saw that his boots were off. They stood in the corner by the door. A mental survey told him that he was lying on his back, covered with a light blanket, which he lifted and saw his belt unbuckled; Nancy made him comfortable.

Hunger pangs churned his stomach,

which motivated him to rise. Fixing his belt and stomping into his boots, he made his way back to the kitchen. Nancy was nowhere to be found, but under a towel on the table, he found a large sliver of apple pie and an empty cup. A glance at the stove located a pot of the dark brew warming near the stove's edge.

'You found the pie,' said Nancy. She stood in the kitchen doorway, smiling as she brushed a sprig of hair from her face.

Beyond her, Jack could see the night. 'You shouldn't have let me sleep so long. It'll be late when I reach the farm.'

'Stay here in John's room. I'm sure Robert wouldn't mind.'

Jack's eyes widened. 'But where will you sleep?'

'I have a room at the boarding house. I couldn't stay here while Mrs Simpson is staying at your place.'

He could feel the blush in his cheeks and hoped it was too dark for her to see. 'Of course,' he said, 'I just thought — '

'I trust Robert well enough, but since we are to be married, I wanted to make sure there would be no gossip from the town.'

'All locked up,' said Robert as he entered the house. He looked at Jack and then Nancy. 'Am I interrupting? I mean, Jack's been away and there's a lot to talk about — '

'No, no, Robert. Please come in, it's your house,' said Nancy.

Robert strolled up to Jack and put his hand on Jack's shoulder, and said, 'We'll all be family soon enough, I reckon.'

Nancy smiled at them both. 'Rebecca runs a tidy house and John's turned into quite the farmer.'

A huge grin filled Robert's face and he twitched his nose. 'That's somethin' I worried would never pass. If there was any good to come of this whole experience, it's John realizin' what Rebecca meant to him and doin' somethin' about it.'

Jack turned to Nancy. 'Have they set a date yet?'

Robert said, 'We all figured it'd be a double wedding soon as you got back — ain't that right, Nancy?'

Nancy looked at Jack as though there was a question in her eyes. 'We haven't worked the details of our arrangement yet.'

'A double wedding tomorrow works for me,' said Jack and he reached out and pulled Nancy to him. Their kiss held a hunger which prolonged their embrace.

'Ahem,' said Robert, who looked away. 'I guess sooner would be better,' he added and began to chuckle.

Jack and Nancy released their embrace; their faces flushed with desire, and their breaths came rapidly and deep.

'Maybe I should fix something for supper,' said Nancy, her voice husky and lacked the conviction of her words. She never broke eye contact with Jack, nor he with her.

Robert, who blushed and continued to look away, said, 'You two have a lot to talk about. I'll make do at the café.' He hurried out before either of them could reply.

Alone, they continued to stare at one another while gaining control of their desires. Jack looked away first. 'I apologize.'

'What for — wanting me? I want you, too.'

'Shall I go find the judge?' asked Jack, and they both laughed, which released the tension they felt.

'I'm tempted, but I think we should wait for a few days at least. Rebecca and I have talked, but nothing specific, and I think you should sort of get her blessing first.'

'I thought it was supposed to be the other way round?'

Nancy's expression sobered. 'You've sprung from nowhere, and she has a father again. Then the turmoil of the kidnapping; now you'd add a step-mother and won't discuss it with her?'

She waited for him to respond. When he didn't she continued. 'That's a lot for a young woman to handle, don't you think?'

Jack smiled. 'She has John. I bet he occupies most of her thoughts. That's what I think.' Nancy's eyes closed to slits, and her hands became planted on her hips. He held up his hands defensively. 'But you're right, I should be more considerate of her feelings. I'll speak with her tomorrow.'

* * *

The next morning, after their breakfast together, Jack rode out to the farm and Rebecca. As he came around the bend, he was surprised to see John with a hoe, earnestly weeding the crops, their roles reversed from weeks earlier.

'So, I never thought I see you behind a plough.' Jack's smile spread into a grin.

John looked up with a sheepish smile. 'Yeah, well — '

Jack interrupted John. 'I'll be calling you son soon, too.'

Still smiling, John shrugged. 'Things change . . . ' Then his expression grew stern. 'How'd it end with McCarthy?'

Looking off into the distance, Jack answered, 'Badly, I wanted to bring him back for trial, but — '

'Dismount and I'll walk you down to the house. Rebecca will want to know you've returned.' His face brightened. 'She'll want to hear your version of how you and Nancy met.'

As if called, Rebecca came out on to the porch. When she saw Jack, she hiked the hem of her skirt, bounded past the steps, and ran to meet them. She hugged him fiercely for several moments. Finally releasing him, she stepped back and asked, 'Are you well — you're not hurt or anything?'

Jack smiled at his daughter. The concern for his wellbeing was evident in her eyes and he experienced the warmth of home. 'I'm fine, daughter. It's you that was in a bad way when last

I saw you.' He held her face in his hands, turning her head to examine her skull. 'You look healed, but are there headaches or dizziness? Head injuries can linger.'

'I'm fine, Father, John and his mother have been spoiling me.'

He tucked her under his arm and continued towards the house. John stood and watched them for several seconds before he returned with his hoe to the field; weeds never stop growing. Jack glanced over his shoulder and saw John's departure.

'The farm seems to be doin' well. I assume that's thanks to John.'

Rebecca squeezed his arm. 'John's been wonderful, Father. It was pretty tough for him at first, but he's a fast learner and a good hand once he put his mind to it. Of course, his mother bein' here to uh . . . guide him has been helpful, too.' They laughed.

As they approached the porch, Sarah Simpson set through the doorway. 'I'm glad to see you've returned all in one piece. Expect you're hungry — how about some pie and coffee?'

Jack's smile was answer enough. He tied the horse and marched into the house. The smell of apple pie and fresh coffee made his mouth water. Sarah and Rebecca busied themselves with his needs.

Two pieces of pie and three cups of coffee later, Jack pushed back from the table. 'Ladies, that pie was awfully good.'

Sarah poured him another cup of coffee. 'Now then, tell us about Nancy Lowe. How did you two meet?'

Rebecca added, 'When did you know you were in love?'

Jack held up his hands to stop the questions. 'I'll tell you about her and me, but first, Rebecca, have I your permission to marry Nancy and bring her here as your stepmother?'

'What? Why would you bother asking my permission? You two are certainly old enough to know your own minds.'

'It's important to Nancy that she

have your blessing.'

Rebecca's eyes watered. A glance at Sarah showed she did as well. Sarah blew her nose on a handkerchief snatched from her sleeve.

'It's so like her to want that.'

'Of course you have my permission. It'll be nice to have another woman around here to talk with and help feed you men.'

'Good. Now that that's settled, I'll tell you about how Nancy and I met.'

What Jack thought should have been a twenty minute story required more than an hour with all their questions and cross-conversation. Finally satisfied that they knew all there was to know about Jack and Nancy's meeting, they sat quietly smiling at each other.

Jack said, 'I'm home now, Sarah. You and John can get back to town and Robert.'

Again the ladies looked at each other and smiled.

'We've made other plans, Jack,' said Sarah.

'Yes,' chimed in Rebecca, 'Sarah and I will go into town to meet with Nancy and plan our weddings. John will stay here with you, and the two of you can work the farm and get to know each other better.' Their expressions told Jack he had no choice.

'Does John know about this plan?' asked Jack.

'He will at lunchtime,' said Rebecca.

A long sigh was all that Jack could manage. Resigned to the situation, he asked, 'How long will the planning take?'

Sarah tapped her finger to her lips as she considered. 'Well, there's the location — out here or in town; town would be better. Then there are the dress fittings, food selection, and refreshments. I'd say at least a week — don't you think, dear?'

Rebecca nodded. 'It's an important event, Father; everything must be perfect. You do understand, don't you?'

She looked so much like her mother with her pinched brow over her large brown eyes and earnest expression, he could refuse her nothing.

'Let's just say I'll go along with your plan, but don't be surprised if you see John and me poking around town.'

19

Page's thoughts were on his business trip to Pittsburg. The oil sample from the farm he took to be analyzed checked out to be pure crude, black gold. Owning that farm would make him a millionaire, maybe the richest man in Texas.

As he walked into the Timber, Page said, 'Whiskey, Sam.'

The bartender poured the drink. 'Glad to see ya back, boss. You're just in time for the big doin's.'

'What are you talking about, Sam?'

'Hadn't ya heard, boss? The Gottlieb girl and her new daddy, Jack McGraw, are gettin' hitched next Saturday.'

His whiskey glass halfway to his lips, Page stared at Sam.

'Somethin' wrong, boss? You don't look too good.'

He'd hoped that Miller and McCarthy would take care of McGraw; maybe even the Simpson kid, too. He knotted back the whiskey.

'Give me that bottle,' he said, and stormed off to his office with the bottle. His problem of one stubborn young girl in his way of a fortune was about to become four people.

After three whiskeys, a plan began to form in his mind. If he got rid of McGraw and the Simpson kid, he'd only have Rebecca to deal with. If she didn't cooperate, then he'd kill her, too.

He'd start with John Simpson. Surely, McGraw and his bride-to-be would hold off their wedding plans to bury the kid. Today was Tuesday; he had three days to make his play.

Rebecca and Nancy shared John's room. They spent their nights, after bedtime, talking and getting to know each other. It wasn't a mother-daughter relationship; rather it was becoming a mentoring friendship. One thing was certain: John and Jack were not going to get away with much.

The first order of business was to

build a separate house for Jack and Nancy, so Rebecca and John could start a family; two boys and two girls at least. They would talk to their husbands-to-be as soon as possible.

★ ★ ★

Morning came and their conversation picked up where it left off with additional input from Sarah.

'For land sakes, you haven't stopped talkin' for days,' Robert said, before he left to open the store.

As he came out of the house, he saw John and Jack rein in their horses at the corral down the way. He walked to meet them.

'Howdy,' he said as he shook hands with Jack. He hugged John. 'I've missed you, son.' Robert held his son at arm's length. 'You've filled out some. Farmin' must agree with you.'

'Yeah, I like it more'n I thought I would. It'll be even better after Rebecca and I are married; she inside?'

Robert shook his head. 'Yes, but I wouldn't bother them just now. They're huddled in there makin' plans.' He pulled out his watch. 'We've got time, let me buy you two a cup of coffee and maybe some pie at the café.'

'Thanks, Robert,' said Jack. 'I can't say we've been enjoying our own cookin' all that much.'

John rolled his eyes. 'That's for damn sure.'

When they walked into the café, Ben Page sat at his usual table finishing his post-breakfast coffee. He nodded. Robert returned the nod; John and Jack ignored him and found a table.

As they waited for their breakfast, they sat and sipped their coffee.

'Their coffee is better'n ours, too,' said Jack.

Robert and John chuckled; their collective mood was lighthearted and humour came easily. Jack looked up and scowled. John glanced over his shoulder and saw Page approaching.

Page gave his best salesman's grin.

'Good morning, gentlemen, it's been a while since you've been to town. I understand congratulations are in order — weddings and all.'

Jack held Page's gaze and nodded. John watched Jack to guide his response. He decided to ignore Page. Until Page put a hand on John's shoulder and said, 'John, no hard feelings about the past. Why don't you and your father-in-law stop by the Timber for a drink? On the house, of course.'

John shrugged off Page's hand and lunged up; his chair slammed into Page's legs. 'Why, you lowlife son of a bitch, hell'll freeze over afore I drink with the likes of you.'

Three things happened nearly simultaneously. John whirled around to attack Page. Robert leaped to his son's defence, and Page thrust his knife aimed at John's heart. Fortunately, for John, Robert placed himself between the two men, and the knife buried itself deep into Robert's ribcage.

It was not a killing blow, but it was

serious. Page stepped back and like a trapped animal, he looked all about the room at the people staring at him.

'It was self-defence — the boy attacked me without provocation.' He struggled to regain his composure. At last, he said, 'Robert Simpson has been hurt — one of you fetch the doctor.'

John knelt by his father, cradling him in his arms. 'I'm sorry, Father, I never meant for you to get hurt.'

Robert Simpson opened his eyes. 'It's not so bad, son. Doc'll fix me up fine. We'll have to postpone the weddings for a week or so, though.'

The relief on John's face spoke volumes for the fear he'd felt when first seeing his father lying on the floor. Until now, Jack had not moved. He stood, his dark eyes hooded as he stared at Page. Unlike John, Jack was heeled and he pulled iron. Page's hands flew up as he began to walk backwards. 'I ain't armed.'

'How am I supposed to believe that when you just stabbed Simpson with a trick-knife from your sleeve? Maybe you got a hideout gun up the other arm. Take off your coat.'

Page hesitated. Jack moved forward and cocked the pistol's hammer. Reluctantly, Page shucked his jacket and revealed a shoulder holster which held a small .32 Colt under his arm.

Jack smiled. 'Unarmed, huh?' He returned his own Remington .44 back to its holster. 'Draw when you're ready.'

'Hold it right there!' said Sheriff Clark. 'I'll shoot the first man to make a move.'

Page said, 'Go ahead and take my gun, Sheriff.'

Clark stepped between Page and McGraw and retrieved the .32.

'What happened?' Clark asked Page.

Page lowered his arms. 'I was giving young Simpson and Mr McGraw my congratulation on their pending nuptials, when the boy attacked me. I defended myself, but Robert got between us. It was an accident that he got hurt.'

Clark looked at the many faces in the café. 'Is that what happened?' He stared at each face one by one and each nodded.

'There's more to it,' said Jack.

'There usually is,' said Clark. With his eyes still on Page, he said, 'Page, you can go for now, but I suggest you don't expect to be invited to the weddings.'

Page stuck out his hand as he looked at his .32 stuffed into Clark's gun belt. 'My revolver?' he asked.

Clark patted the weapon. 'I'll just hang on to it for now.'

Page stooped, picked up his jacket and backed out of the café. 'You haven't heard the last of this, Clark, or you either, McGraw.' Outside, after several deep breaths, he put on his jacket, and he regretted his outburst.

Doctor Benson strolled through the front door just after Page left. He saw Robert Simpson on the floor with the knife protruding from his back. His glance gravitated to McGraw, and he said, 'Smart thinkin' to leave it alone.'

'Somethin' I learned in the War,' said Jack.

Doc Benson surveyed the room and

pointed at a couple of men. 'You two get Simpson over to my office.'

Simpson was trying to stand. 'That's all right, Doc. I can walk if John'll help me.'

Jack stepped in and helped Robert to his feet and careful not to aggravate the wound, held him up under the arm. 'Let me, I know how, I've helped plenty to aid stations.'

John followed along behind them carrying his father's things. Robert said, 'Son, you'd better go tell your mother. Make sure she understands it ain't bad. I'll be home after a while.'

John looked at Doc Benson. 'It'll be more like morning, but he'll be fine. Your ma can come over whenever she wishes.'

After John broke the news to his mother, Rebecca stayed with John to console him. Nancy went to Sarah to comfort her and see for herself that Jack was indeed not harmed.

At least I've delayed the weddings, thought Page. How was he to get rid of

McGraw and his daughter? He could ambush McGraw; folks would believe he had enemies, and it was them who'd done the deed. The girl was another story. Without her father, would she continue at the farm, or marry young Simpson and move into town and work at his father's store?

He smacked his fist into the palm of the other hand.

'I can't risk it,' he said aloud and poured another whiskey.

The bottle was nearly empty. Holding it up to inspection, he decided he was drinking too much and then, he turned and opened the cabinet behind his desk and withdrew a fresh bottle.

The more he drank, the more he liked the idea of killing McGraw and blaming it on McCarthy's kin. He'd kill them both, but how?

* * *

The next morning, Page rode east out of town, heading for Shreveport. He knew of a man there, who for the right amount of money would not hesitate to kill a woman.

At the saloons by the docks, Page made the rounds. His questions were discreetly asked. It was late in the evening of his second day, when a grey-haired bearded man slid into the chair opposite his place at the table.

The man's smell from his filth was only surpassed by the ghastly odour from his breath. The few teeth he still possessed were broken and rotted.

'Here tell you been askin' for me.'

Page flinched at the putrid breath wafting from the man as he spoke. 'If you're the one they call Swamp-man Monroe, I am.'

'I been called that afore. What're ya wantin'?'

Page looked around to see if anyone watched; to the contrary the other patrons placed their stares elsewhere. Monroe's reputation was well-known by those who frequented the docks.

20

When Page returned, Robert Simpson, though still under the doctor's care, was up and about, attending to his store. Nancy and John did the work, but Robert was there to watch, which seemed to make him happier.

'It makes the day go by sooner,' he said.

No one except Sam seemed to notice when Page returned. 'Where ya been, boss? You didn't leave no word. I was gettin' worried.'

Page glared at Sam. 'You didn't say anything to anyone, did ya?'

'Why no, boss. I know you keep your goings and comings to yourself. I just didn't know where ya was and started to get worried — that's all.'

The saloon was empty, but still he leaned across the bar close to Sam. In a low voice, he said, 'Anyone asks, I've been here all along — you got that?'

Sam stared at Page's eyes, they didn't seem normal. Dark circles around blood-shot orbs; the boss needed some rest.

'Sure thing, boss,' Sam smiled reassuringly. 'You need some sleep. I'll take care of things out here.'

Page glanced in the mirror behind Sam, and saw his reflection. He looked ghastly; dirty, rumpled, and obviously he'd had no sleep for days.

'You're right, Sam.' Page numbly walked into his office, closing the door behind him. Once inside, he dropped on to the sofa and slept without moving for six hours.

Later, after going to his room for a bath and change of clothes, Page made his appearance in the Timber Saloon. For the next three days and nights, he made it a point for the folks of Crockett to know his whereabouts.

The double wedding was rescheduled for the upcoming weekend. Rebecca and Jack were to come into town the day before, so she, and he, could prepare for their nuptials. After the weddings, John and Rebecca would be going by train to San Francisco; it was a wedding present from John's parents.

Nancy and Jack planned to return to the farm, and finish the small house Jack was building for them. He expected to have it completed and to be moved in before Rebecca and John returned.

Moods were high; the whole town looked forward to the celebration to come. No one paid much attention to an old smelly trapper hanging around the stable, though he made it a point to tell a few people his name was McCarthy.

It was early; Rebecca couldn't sleep, so she was up early preparing breakfast. Jack yawned as he entered the kitchen.

'You're certainly up early — couldn't sleep?'

Rebecca smiled at her father. The twinkle in her eyes conveyed that she was only mildly distressed she'd been so noisy.

'Sorry, Father, but tomorrow's the wedding, and we've so much to do,

Nancy and I.' She poured him coffee and then returned to the stove and started breakfast. 'I didn't sleep at all.'

'I'll go do my chores while you're fixin' breakfast. When we've eaten, I'll hitch the team while you're packing.'

Rebecca began to hum softly as Jack left the house. Outside, halfway across the yard towards the barn, Jack halted. Something wasn't right; it was too quiet. The chickens were still on their roosts; the horses acted nervous and pranced wide-eyed about the corral, looking for an opportunity to escape. They acted like a bad storm was about to blow, but when he looked up at the sky it was a clear blue Texas morning. It couldn't be more beautiful, however, there was still something amiss. He shook his head and chuckled. It's the pre-wedding jitters, he thought. After, he attended to his chores, including feeding the chickens — Rebecca's job — he hitched up the wagon.

When he stopped the wagon at the porch, Rebecca stood waiting. As he climbed the steps, she said, 'There's more luggage than I expected.' Her eyes pleaded forgiveness.

Jack smiled at her and peered inside. 'As I recall, it's less than your mother packed when we got hitched.' He lugged out three pieces, and added, ''Course, you've got to convince John and the stage line that you need all this.' He turned his face so she couldn't see his grin.

She smiled. 'John won't be a problem. Do you really think the stage line will complain?'

Jack's face beamed with laughter. 'Maybe not the driver, but his horses will have somethin' to say for sure.'

Rebecca laughed with him. Finally, she sighed. 'I'll get Sarah and Nancy to help me and see what I can leave behind.'

He helped her on to the wagon, and looked around the farm once more. Things should be all right for two days, but still he worried. 'Hold tight, sweetheart, I want to check the house again.'

Rebecca called to his back as he entered the house. 'You worry too much. We need to get started, people are waiting.'

Stepping through the door, he turned and pulled it closed. He turned the key in the lock.

'Don't know why I bother, if someone wants in, they'll just force the door or break a window.'

'Locks aren't for thieves, Father. They're to help good folks to remain honest — haven't you ever heard that?'

'A time or two, daughter, a time or two.'

With a slap of the reins, the horses leaned in their harnesses, pulled the wagon out of the yard and up the low grade towards the rise. Beyond the rise was the road to Crockett.

A mile further towards town, the horse on the left collapsed like a poleaxed-steer. Before the animal's action registered on Jack's mind, he heard the explosion of a large calibre rifle. It was a distinctive noise. One he had not heard since the War. It's a sniper, he thought, and without further consideration, he threw himself across the wagon's seat, diving for the ground, dragging Rebecca with him.

Fortunately for Rebecca, she was caught completely off guard, and tumbled with her father without resisting. When they stopped, she asked, 'What happened, Father?' and tried to rise.

Jack reached out and pulled her back down. 'Stay put! Someone's tryin' to kill us, or at least me.'

'What? I mean, was that a gun shot?'

'He killed the horse to stop the wagon. I dragged us off the seat before he could take another shot.' Jack surveyed their surroundings, and pointed. 'See those trees beyond the brush?' She nodded. 'I want you to crawl through there without disturbing anything, if you can. When you get into the trees, head south towards town. Maybe someone will have heard the shot and will be coming to investigate.'

As he spoke, his eyes scanned across the road. 'What are you going to do?'

There was a distinct urgency in her voice.

With a smile meant to reassure his daughter, he said, 'I'm goin' over there and teachin' him some manners.'

Rebecca paled and her eyes widened. 'But you don't even have a revolver. Come with me and we'll get to town together.'

He patted her hand. 'If we both go for the woods, he'll just track us and — ' His eyes turned back across the road. 'This is best, Rebecca. I've dealt with snipers before; I'm still here.'

Her eyes began to tear. 'But — '

'It'll be fine. I'm goin' to unhitch the other horse and when it gets to town, someone's sure to recognize her and come out here to see what's wrong. You watch for 'em and warn 'em when they come. It's time, get to movin'.'

Rebecca dried her eyes and readied herself for the task at hand. On her hands and knees, she picked her way through the brush headed for the trees beyond.

While Rebecca made her way to the trees, Jack inched towards the horse. He stayed close to the ground and moved slowly. As he approached the mare, he began speaking in a low, reassuring tone. If the shooter suspected what Jack was about to do, he'd shoot the mare.

The reins hung loose and didn't present a problem. He eased the trace chains from the tree hooks, but the horses were connected by the neck yoke. Like an anchor, it held the mare, allowing her no advance movement. Jack belly crawled to the horse's front legs and waited for several minutes. He wanted Rebecca to be in the trees before his next move.

Rebecca moved slowly, trying not to disturb the bushes. Regardless, Jack saw occasional movement, but it wasn't enough, he hoped, to catch the shooter's attention.

It was time; Jack stood, keeping next to the mare's legs to conceal his. He flipped open his pocket knife and hesitated. It was his only weapon, and he would lose it after he cut the yoke loose from the mare. Jack gripped the mare's bridle with his left and reached under her neck with his right.

The leather was taut and Jack's knife was sharp. A single slash with the blade and the mare was free. She bristled against Jack's restraint, but he held firm. Dropping the knife, he slung himself up and on to the horse's back and put his heels to her flanks. She didn't require much encouragement; Jack nearly fell when she propelled forward like a shot from a cannon.

Jack leaned close to her back. The expected shot came, but missed. The shooter hadn't expected Jack's single escape, and had to adjust his aim for a snap shoot, which was no easy task with a big bore rifle.

Around the bend, and free from the shooter's sight, Jack gathered the reins and brought the mare to a halt. He slid off her back, quickly bundled the reins into the harness, and slapped the horse's rump, sending her at a run towards Crockett — and help. Scanning the trees to his left, he selected a route into the trees. He intended to take on his would-be assassin.

★ ★ ★

Monroe's first shot killed the horse, but quick as he was, he couldn't reload fast enough to match McGraw's response. He'd ambushed many men this way. He shot their horse and while they're trying to figure out what's happened, he shot them dead.

A grin crossed his face. I underestimated McGraw, he thought, but it won't happen again. With his Sharps .50 calibre pointed towards the bushes past the wagon, he watched for movement.

A bush moved, but then nothing further. He thought about sending another shot into the brush, but that would give McGraw a few seconds of advantage; he wouldn't underestimate him again. He saw, or sensed movement at the tree line. Then he saw the colour of Rebecca's clothing. Finally, he had a target.

He repositioned his rifle's support and settled to take his shot. The distance was beyond a carbine's range, but not for his Sharps .50, it would be easy for him.

Focused on the girl, the subtle movement at the wagon went unnoticed. When the horse bolted with McGraw on its back, he snapped shot at him without thinking. McGraw and the horse were out of sight by the time he reloaded, and realized, he should have shot the horse. When he looked for the girl she too was gone.

'Thin' you're purdy slick don't ya, McGraw? Well, you won't get away next time — that's a promise.' His was a lonely business, and he often spoke to himself. Monroe didn't mind, though, there was no one he liked better than himself.

* * *

The skills a man learns to survive in battle are slow to leave, if ever. Years of playing chess with Kurt kept Jack's mind sharp; sharp enough he hoped to outwit his assassin.

He smelled the shooter before he actually saw him, which meant he was down wind, so his horse wouldn't give him away. As he moved through the cover, Jack found two fist-size rocks. Stealth and those two stones were his only weapons.

Jack peered down on the man who faced the road beyond. He had a spy glass to his eye, and he scanned the tree line on the far side. Looking for Rebecca, thought Jack, well, he'll never get another shot. With a rock held firmly in each hand, Jack stood and started down the hillside.

The sound of a breaking twig, or who knows what, caused the shooter to momentarily freeze. Without warning, he fell to his right, swinging the huge gun around to fire on Jack.

Jack let sail a rock, which caused the

man to cover his head and lose sight of Jack. That was all the time Jack needed; he was on the man in an instant. Jack couldn't contain the fury of his rage as he repeatedly slammed the rock into the man's ugly, smelly face. At last, the man's body went limp.

When he looked down, the man was a bloody pulp, but he still breathed. While the man was unconscious, Jack tied him to the horse and made his way back to the wagon. His calls for Rebecca went unanswered. She's safe, he thought . . . he hoped.

After he dumped the unconscious man into the wagon bed, Jack hitched the man's horse to the wagon. It was a jury-rigged affair, but it would serve his purpose. As the wagon limped towards town, he called Rebecca's name every few minutes. Close to a half hour down the road, Jack heard a response.

'Here! Father, I'm here.'

Jack halted and jumped down from the wagon. He fiercely embraced his daughter. 'Are you all right, Rebecca? I was so worried.' He held her at arm's length for a quick examination and then hugged her again, tighter than before.

'Father, please, I can't breathe.' He released her, but it was plain on his face that it was not of his choice.

'Sorry.' His concerned expression was replaced with a sheepish grin. 'Fathers are allowed to worry.'

Rebecca glanced at the strange horse. 'Are you all right? What happened back there? I heard another shot.'

'I captured the shooter. He's in our wagon, but I gotta warn you, as bad as he looks, he smells worse.'

Halfway towards town, they heard horses galloping towards them. Based on the size of the dust cloud, it was several riders. John led the group by two full horse lengths. He was out of the saddle before his horse stopped, and he lifted Rebecca down from the wagon and held her tightly in his arms.

Jack looked on for a few seconds. 'She told me she didn't like to be squeezed so tight.'

John glanced up at Jack, his brow pinched as he loosened his embrace. 'Jack?'

'Oh, Father's being a nuisance,' said Rebecca. 'He nearly crushed my ribcage after the ambush.'

'Ambush?' asked John.

Clark moved near the wagon and looked down. 'Is this the owl hoot that tried to bushwhack you?'

Jack nodded. 'He killed my horse with that Sharps and then went after us. We bailed from the wagon before he got off another shot.'

'Your other horse came running into town like her tail was afire,' said Clark. 'John here lit out before the rest of us could find our animals.' He winked at Jack. 'He must've been worried about you, Jack.'

Monroe moaned and then tried to move. Only one eye would open as the other was swollen shut. 'What happened?' he asked.

'You picked the wrong man to ambush. Who hired you?' questioned

Clark. 'I got a pretty good idea who, but you could make it easier on yourself if you confirmed who it was.'

Realization came into Monroe's eye. 'I ain't sayin' nothin'.'

'Suit yourself, but you're lookin' at twenty years,' said Clark. 'It don't seem fair to see you serve it by yourself.'

Monroe continued to glare.

★ ★ ★

John held Rebecca in his lap and started back to town. Clark added his horse to the makeshift team and rode with McGraw on the wagon.

'You know who's behind all this, don't you?' said Jack, loud enough for Monroe to listen. 'If this bushwhacker don't talk, then Page will get away clean.'

'Well, least you won't have to worry about this fellow for a good long while. Huntsville's full of hard cases like him.'

21

Page paced the floor. Periodically, he stopped and looked through the window from his upstairs apartment. The commotion caused by McGraw's horse running wild through town, engendered in him the thought that McGraw and his daughter were dead.

At the sound of people gathering on the street, he peered once more out the window; his jaw clenched.

'Damn, he's still alive. What will it take to kill that man?'

Then he saw Monroe sprawled in the back of the wagon. The flush of anger drained and a fear grabbed his gut as he wondered if he lived.

The wagon stopped at Doc's office, and they carried Monroe inside. He saw Clark motion to his deputy to guard the prisoner. Page's pacing resumed, this time filled with worry. He stopped and went to the window and watched. Neither Clark nor anyone else headed for his apartment. So, Monroe didn't talk, he thought. Maybe he wasn't able, but once they get him inside a jail cell it might be a different story.

'I know it's early, McGraw, but I could do with a stiff drink,' said Clark. He glanced at the Timber as he spoke.

'Not yet. I've got to see Nancy — '

'I'm here, Jack.'

He turned around just in time for Nancy to throw her arms around his neck and bury her face under his chin. Though muffled, he heard her say, 'When your horse tore into town like that, and John rushed out to find Rebecca, I panicked. Jack, darling, the thought of losing you is unbearable.'

Jack pulled her free of his neck. 'Well, I'm OK and so is Rebecca. I don't want to let this . . . this incident change our wedding plans.' He glanced at the wagon. 'Rebecca needs help decidin' on what to take to Frisco.'

Clark said, 'You two go on over to

Simpson's place. I'll bring along the wagon.'

Jack tucked Nancy under his arm, and guided her towards Simpson's store. 'You shouldn't fret so, Nancy. Why, this time tomorrow we'll be hitched — Mister and Missus.'

John and Rebecca waited on the porch with John's mother when Jack and Nancy walked past the store. They noticed Rebecca wore a clean dress, and her pale face had regained its nature rosy color. Clark and the wagon followed.

When Sarah saw the stack of luggage, she said, 'Child, you can't take all that to San Francisco. You're just visitin', not movin'.' All but Rebecca laughed.

'Well, I just didn't — '

Nancy interrupted, 'Don't worry, Rebecca. Sarah and I will help you get it all sorted out before tomorrow.'

Clark and John unloaded the wagon while Jack stayed with Nancy and Rebecca. His reassuring manner readily calmed them. When they'd finished,

Clark gave Jack a nod. 'I need to go with Clark to file a report about what happened. I'll be back soon.'

'Can't that wait?' asked Nancy. 'You have him in custody.'

Jack smiled patiently. 'I'll be back soon enough, besides you ladies have chores of your own, and you don't want us men around.' He winked at John.

Nancy glanced at the luggage, and saw Rebecca and Sarah lugging it into the house. 'Oh all right, you win. I'll see you later, but please don't be too long.'

Agreeing, Jack motioned to John and Clark. The three went to Clark's office. Once inside, Jack said, 'If you're like most sheriffs, there's a bottle in one of those drawers. I'll take that stiff drink now.'

'I hate bein' predictable,' said Clark. 'I keep it in the ammo draw under the long guns — it's not so handy that way.'

John rustled three cups and placed them on the desk. Clark poured ample portions and sat back in his chair, taking the first sip. 'What are you plannin' to do about Page?' he asked.

'You're the sheriff, Clark, you tell me,' said Jack.

'Without proof he hired that fella, there ain't nothin' legal can be done, which aggravates me to no end.'

'Why can't you make him talk?' asked John.

'Can't make a man talk if he don't want to,' said Clark.

'But — ' said Jack as he stared through the window at Doc's office. 'When can you move him from Doc's to here?'

'Um, you beat him pretty bad, Jack. Not that I'm complainin', he deserved everythin' he got. What've you got on your mind?'

John moved to the edge of his seat as he and Clark waited for Jack to speak. Jack stopped rubbing his chin and turned. 'After that fella comes to, we march him over here, plain as day and lock him up. We'll wait, say half an hour and then go and arrest Page for questioning. Once we get him in here, we stand him in front of the shooter's cell and ask, 'This the one?''

'I get it,' said John. 'You figure Page will say something that will show he's been behind everything.'

Jack nodded and turned to Clark. The sheriff poured a second whiskey and pushed the bottle forward to the edge of the desk.

'It might just work, but what if it don't?'

'Well . . . ' Jack paused to grab the bottle. 'I guess I could refuse to press charges if he'd testify to who paid 'im.'

John, who sat quietly in his chair, suddenly spoke. 'Don't say nothin' to Page. Just put them in the same cell and then offer not to press charges and see what happens.'

Clark and Jack exchanged glances and then looked back at John. 'Why, that's a hell of an idea,' said Jack, and he raised his cup in a mock salute.

Soon after they brought Monroe into town, Page sat at his desk drinking whiskey. Sam provided food, but he felt no appetite. The tension of not knowing and having to wait took its toll. For the hundredth time, he rose to pace the floor. He stopped to examine his reflection in the mirror by the door.

The stranger who stared back startled him. His bloodshot eyes were sunken into dark circles; hair normally coiffed deranged, skin ashen, and his beard stubbly. It suddenly occurred to him that maybe, just maybe, he should have given up when Billy and Frank were killed. If he was dead, or in prison, the oil wouldn't do him any good then.

He jumped at the knock on the door. 'Who is it?'

The door swung open and as Sam stuck his head through, he said, 'It's me, boss, Sam.' He noticed the food on Page's desk was untouched. 'You should eat somethin', boss.'

'What do you want, Sam, can't you see I'm busy?'

Sam retreated, and then returned. 'Sheriff Clark's here and wants to see ya. He says its official.'

Page stiffened; his eyes hardened. 'Tell him to come back later, I'm too busy to see him now.'

The door closed, and Page returned to his desk and the near empty bottle. Glass in hand, he sloshed its content on his front as the office door slammed open, making him jump. Clark filled the doorway with his hand on the butt of his Colt.

'You're comin' with me. There are some questions that need answerin'.'

Sitting down his glass, Page stood. He slowly opened his jacket to expose his waist. 'I'm not armed, Clark.'

Clark stepped back, but kept his hand on his Colt.

Page smoothed his coat, finger-combed his hair, and rubbed his face to bring back some colour. 'Where to, Sheriff?'

'We're goin' to my office. I've got a prisoner for you to meet.'

His expression sobered for a split-second, then he replied, 'How interesting, Sheriff. Is it anyone I know?'

Clark chuckled. 'We think so . . . '

''We'?' asked Page. 'Who else is involved?'

'Give it up, Page, we know it was you.'

Page knew Clark was bluffing. If he really had any evidence, he would have arrested him outright instead of this charade. If he bluffed in return, they couldn't prove a thing against him.

'There you go with that 'We' again. Just what is it, Sheriff, that you think I've been up to?'

Clark didn't reply, which caused Page to smile; he was correct. They were bluffing and would lose.

* * *

Inside the jail, Monroe lay on his bunk. Only the man's smell and ragged appearance alerted Page that it was Monroe. Part of his face was bandaged and the rest purple and yellow. It was clear that McGraw had nearly killed the assassin.

Clark swung open the door and

shoved Page into the cell with Monroe. 'Sheriff, you can't put me in here with him. I demand a separate cell — as far away as possible.'

'What's the matter, don't you like to associate with your employees? He don't seem to mind,' said Jack, who entered unannounced. Page's eyes jerked up when he heard Jack's voice.

'Monroe is not in my employ!' said Page.

Clark and Jack exchanged glances and smiled. 'So that's his name; he wouldn't tell us. So, how do you know it, Page?'

Page's eyes darted between Clark and McGraw. Finally, he said, 'He was in the Timber a few days back.'

Clark nodded. 'That so? Should be easy enough to confirm. He's not the type of *hombre* a fella forgets meeting.'

Quickly, too quickly to sound convincing, Page said, 'It was early, Sam was in the back. Monroe left before he returned.'

'How convenient. Still, someone else

must've seen him around town. I'll ask about, there are folks routinely up early.'

Page shrugged. 'Do as you please, but that's the only time I have seen Monroe until today.'

Monroe watched and listened to Page and his jailers. During the latter part of the conversation, he rose and stood behind Page. He stared hard with what was left of his good eye. Jack glanced past Page, drawing Page's attention to Monroe. Page whirled around and took a guarded stance. Monroe didn't react.

'What've you got to say, Monroe?' asked Jack. 'You're lookin' at twenty years at Huntsville Prison for attempted murder.'

Monroe continued to stare at Page with his one good eye.

'It was an accident that I shot your horse. I'll pay for the horse, and no hard feelin's about this.' Monroe gestured towards his face. 'I weren't much to look at afore, maybe this'll improve my looks some.' He tried to laugh, but flinched with pain instead.

'That don't account for the second shot and the fight when I circled round behind you.' Monroe shrugged.

'I'll tell you what I'm offering, Monroe,' said Jack. 'If you'll testify against Page, I'll drop all charges against you and let you go free after the trial. What do you say to that offer?'

Monroe's good eye lit up. He looked at the sheriff. 'That legal, Sheriff? I turn on Page and I walk free?'

A genuine smile creased Clark's face. 'Unless you're wanted somewhere else — '

The hint of a smile appeared on Monroe's torn and bruised face. 'I ain't wanted. I'll tell you what you want to know.'

'Shut up, fool.' Page trembled with rage. 'I'll get us the best lawyer money can buy and they'll never convict us. Just keep quiet, you imbecile!'

Monroe's good eye squinted. 'Maybe's I's ain't too smart, but I knows I don't need you to get out of here.' He gave Page a shove and stepped to the bars. 'Sheriff — ' Monroe gave out a groan, clutched the bars and sagged to the floor. Page stood behind the body with a bloody knife in hand.

Clark pulled his Colt. 'Drop the knife, or I'll shoot.'

Page's rage subsided and he began to pale. 'You saw him, Sheriff, he attacked me. I had to defend myself.'

'I won't tell you again, Page. Drop the knife and step back.'

He thumbed the Colt's hammer, and the sound of the cylinder ratcheting got through to Page where Clark's words failed. He dropped the knife and moved away from it and Monroe's body.

★   ★   ★

Nearly the whole town turned out for the wedding reception held behind the church. There weren't many weddings and it was the town's first double ceremony. Tomorrow, John and Rebecca were catching the morning stage to start their honeymoon; less several pieces of luggage. Jack and Nancy were going home to the farm and to start building their house.

The four of them stood by while the townsfolk filed by, shaking the grooms' hands and kissing the brides. Clark was at the end of the line. He had a bottle of brandy cradled in the crook of his arm. 'I thought you could use a pick me up just about now?'

Jack glanced at Nancy, who smiled. 'Go ahead — I want to visit Sarah and the others anyway.'

Jack and Clark sat on one of the picnic tables under a live oak. Clark passed Jack the brandy and he took a long pull. 'It's been a long day. Hell, it's been a long few days. Hear anything back from up north?'

A huge grin grew on Clark's face. 'It appears you're about to become a gentleman farmer.'

Jack passed back the brandy and cocked his head. 'That so?'

Lowering the bottle, Clark said, 'I got answers back from the folks in Philadelphia. The oil sample Page gave them to examine is of high quality and there are people in the oil business that want to speak with you and Rebecca. That craggy part of the farm is goin' to make you rich.'

Nancy walked up and stood by her husband. 'Rich?' she asked.

Jack gave a laugh as he hugged his wife and stared out across the crowd at his daughter. 'I don't see how I could get any richer than I am now.'

We do hope that you have enjoyed reading this large print book.

Did you know that all of our titles are available for purchase?

We publish a wide range of high quality large print books including:
Romances, Mysteries, Classics
General Fiction
Non Fiction and Westerns

Special interest titles available in large print are:
The Little Oxford Dictionary
Music Book, Song Book
Hymn Book, Service Book

Also available from us courtesy of Oxford University Press:
Young Readers' Dictionary
(large print edition)
Young Readers' Thesaurus
(large print edition)

For further information or a free brochure, please contact us at:
Ulverscroft Large Print Books Ltd.,
The Green, Bradgate Road, Anstey,
Leicester, LE7 7FU, England.
Tel: (00 44) **0116 236 4325**
Fax: (00 44) **0116 234 0205**

Other titles in the
Linford Western Library:

THE LAW IN CROSSROADS

J. L. Guin

Jack Bonner, former lawman, has retired to the small town of Crossroads, Texas. But when a rogue gunman shoots up a saloon, Bonner feels obligated to investigate, as there is no lawman in town. He reluctantly agrees to take on temporary marshal duties. Things go sour when Z Bar ranch owner Horace Davies hires a known gunman instead of cowboys, turning the Z Bar into a haven for outlaws. And when Davies offers a reward for Bonner's demise, Jack goes into action . . .

ALL MUST DIE

I. J. Parnham

Ten years ago, a spree of murders shocked the townsfolk of Monotony. The victims were shot and dumped, with words scrawled on the ground beside them. When Sykes Caine was arrested for a bank raid, the killings stopped ... Now Sheriff Cassidy Yates must deal with a perplexing case. A man is shot to death — and words are scratched into the ground by the corpse. With Sykes now released from jail and back in town, the finger of suspicion is pointed squarely at him ...

LONELY IS THE GUNFIGHTER

Steve Hayes

Morgan 'Coop' Cooper is a man with a tragic past and an uncertain future. Drifting into the town of Rocas Rojas, his trail crosses with that of enigmatic saloon owner Lorna Rutledge. They hit it off immediately — but there is more to Lorna than meets the eye. Almost before he knows it, Coop finds himself teamed up with a gunman named Gospel Curtis, and robbing a gold train at Deep River Gorge . . .

THE WIDELOOPERS

Corba Sunman

Tod Bailey rides out of Dodge City a happy man. He has sold his herd, and the only job remaining before collecting his payment is to deliver the beef to the buyer's corrals. But his cheerful mood will not last long. Upon his arrival back at camp, he is greeted with utter chaos: his animals have been stolen by rustlers, his pard Packy Lambert has been killed, and his younger brother Thad is dying with a bullet in his chest . . .